SLEIGHT
OF BODY

Ralph McInerny

M
MACMILLAN
LONDON

First published in the United States of America under the title *Abracadaver*

First published in the United Kingdom 1989 by
MACMILLAN LONDON LIMITED
4 Little Essex Street London WC2R 3LF
and Basingstoke

Associated companies in Auckland, Delhi, Dublin, Gaborone,
Hamburg, Harare, Hong Kong, Johannesburg, Kuala Lumpur,
Lagos, Manzini, Melbourne, Mexico City, Nairobi, New York,
Singapore and Tokyo

ISBN 0-333-51785-7

A CIP catalogue record for this book is available from the British Library

Printed and bound in Great Britain
by The Camelot Press Ltd, Southampton

For Cathy and Mike Brownell

One

Seated behind the dozen old people who had braved the wintry weather to enjoy "An Evening of Magic with Father Don," Roger Dowling marveled at his classmate's skill. There were those who said it had taken magic to get Don Schneider through the seminary, but Roger suspected it had been a combination of faith and determination. Like most people, Roger Dowling was confident he would be able to detect how a magician creates his illusions, but for the life of him he did not see how Don was producing flowers from midair, multicolored cloths from one plain handkerchief, and fairly minting half dollars from his ear. A squeal went up as Don stepped toward his meager but appreciative audience and found a live hamster atop the head of Aggie Miller. Don slipped the little beast into his coat pocket and bowed to the applause.

The show had been scheduled to begin at 8:00, but because of the snow Roger Dowling had held it back until 8:30 when it was clear that the blizzard had decided most of those who frequented the St. Hilary's parish center to remain in the warmth of their homes. His introduction of Father Don had been half apology and half anticipatory praise.

"That's my first trick," Don said, "making my audience disappear. Perhaps I can remedy that before the night is through."

Thank God, the few that had come were delighted with Don's magic. He could certainly not have received a better reception, no matter how large the crowd. As it was, there were exactly eleven old people watching Don like a hawk—seven of them women, seated in chairs that during the day supported them at bridge tables.

"How did you do that, Father?" Aggie Miller asked. "How did you find a hamster in my hair?"

Don waggled a finger at her and smiled. "Now, madam, a magician never divulges his tricks."

"Where is the hamster now?" Edna Hospers asked, as caught up in the show as any of the old people who were her charges at the center.

Instead of answering, Don kicked off a loafer, stooped down and pulled out a hamster. The audience was astounded, and after a moment of startled silence they burst into their most enthusiastic applause of the night. Don could not have been more pleased.

"For my next trick, I need your cooperation. Does anyone have a piece of precious jewelry he is willing to risk?"

He looked around but there was reluctance of a friendly kind until Aggie Miller, having looked to her right and then to her left, satisfied that no one was going to volunteer, stood up.

"You can use this ring," she said, and began to twist it with exaggerated effort. "It's really too small."

"Take your time," Don said.

Fred called from the back. "Can't you remove it with magic?"

The others were not amused. They understood that their complicity was needed if the magic show was to work. Fortunately Aggie got the ring off her finger and handed it to Don, who bowed in gratitude while whipping from somewhere on his person a large white silk handkerchief, into which he placed the ring with exaggerated and deliberate motions. When he had it packaged neatly, he turned around. When he faced them again, he was holding a hammer and wearing a devilish expression. He crouched and put the folded handkerchief on the floor where everyone could see it, and began to hit it ferociously with the hammer. Aggie gasped and the others looked amazed. Don stopped and looked at Aggie.

"I hope it wasn't your best ring."

The expression on Aggie's face was eloquent; Don looked abject. He picked up the handkerchief, stood up, and began carefully to unfold it. As he did so rose petals fell from it, and when it was completely open the audience could see a diminutive flowerpot with a now-denuded rose in it.

It was a triumph: applause, comments on the trick, joking of the kind that goes with having been fooled, and above all this, the wail of Aggie Miller.

"Where is my ring? Where is my ring?"

The others fell quiet and identified themselves with Aggie's question, looking expectantly at Don. He in turn looked at them with surprise.

"You want the ring back?"

Aggie insisted that it was a good ring, not junk jewelry at all, and of course she wanted it back.

"I wish you had told me that earlier," Don said, and he appeared to be genuinely upset.

"But where is it?"

"You saw it turn into a rose," Don replied.

But he was a practiced entertainer and knew that it was unwise to tease his audience too much. He picked up one of the rose pedals and examined it thoroughly, while every other eye in the room did the same. A moment later Don stepped up to Edna Hospers and seemed to pull a ring from her finger. He stepped back, holding it up and peering inside.

"Aha. There is an inscription. To FG from AG. *Con amore.* Is this your ring, madam?"

"That's mine," Aggie said, beaming. She took the ring from Don and joined in the applause that did not drown out Fred's question. "Who's AG and FG?"

"None of your business," Aggie said mysteriously.

It was another twenty minutes before Roger Dowling and his guest went along a shoveled walk from the school to the rectory where Marie Murkin had hot cocoa ready for them.

"You should have come, Marie," Roger Dowling said. "It was a wonderful show."

She sighed. "I couldn't leave the rectory empty."

Like many housekeepers, Marie Murkin considered herself to be in charge of the parish. She had been in her post years before Roger Dowling had been assigned as pastor of St. Hilary's, but she was hardly a nuisance. Roger Dowling considered her indispensable to the smooth running of the parish, and she, in a moment of weakness, had said to Phil Keegan that Father Dowling was the best pastor the parish had ever seen.

"Father Schneider makes things appear and disappear at will, Marie."

"Is that right? How about making the snow disappear?"

"The Lord and I have an agreement. He takes care of the weather and I take care of . . ." He pulled a quarter from Marie's ear. "This sort of thing."

Marie stepped back openmouthed. She looked from Don to Roger Dowling and back again. The pastor half expected her to sprinkle their guest with holy water.

"Now, if only I could do that, we could stop taking up the collection," Roger Dowling said.

"Good heavens, I nearly forgot, Father. Mrs. Loring called to ask if you could come see her father. Apparently he has taken a turn for the worse. I promised to pass on the message and I have."

Mrs. Loring's father, old Willis Wirth, had terminal cancer

and Marie was convinced that the family wanted others to do their duty for them. She was wrong. It was Willis who insisted the priest come, and Roger Dowling felt no inclination to deny the request. Willis Wirth, to the dismay of his family, had become a Catholic at the age of seventy-two after an acquisitive and irreligious life had left him wealthy but wondering, at last, what it all meant. Soon now he would know, and Roger Dowling was ready to give him all the comfort he could, as a priest and as a friend.

"Where is he?" Don asked.

"Riverview."

Don nodded. "I hear it's very nice."

Riverview was the most elegant and expensive retirement facility Fox River possessed, and Willis was receiving the most sophisticated medical attention possible. But his illness was now far out of the reach of the doctors.

"Can I drop you off, Roger?"

"Thanks, Don. I better take my car. I don't know how long I'll be there, and getting a cab requires something more than magic after midnight."

"I wish you'd take a cab both ways," Marie said. "Listen to that."

Outside the wind wailed, meaning the snow that had been falling all afternoon would begin to drift. It was not a night on which one would choose to go out, but if Don could brave it to put on a magic show for some elderly parishioners, Roger Dowling felt he could do the same to provide consolation to a dying man.

Wearing a fur-lined car coat and a cap, Roger Dowling went outside with Don.

"Thanks so much for doing the show, Don. They really loved it. So did I. You're very good."

"Practice," Don said, embarrassed by the praise.

"Come back soon when we can just sit and talk."

"I'd like that, Roger."

The wind whipped at them, driving snow before it. It was neither the time nor the place to prolong a conversation. The two priests shook hands. Roger Dowling trudged to the garage where he pumped the gas once and turned the key, and the motor roared to life. It seemed a night for magic.

AG to FG. *Con amore.*

The inscription Don had read from Aggie's ring stuck in his head like an unwanted tune. Had Aggie's maiden name begun with a *G*? But he knew she was a Riley. Besides, AG was the giver.

. And then a name formed in his mind. He peered ahead where his headlights seemed to confer vitality on the falling snow.

What a coincidence. Of course it couldn't be. But then he said the name aloud.

Frances Grice.

She had been missing since fall; just disappeared one day without a trace, without any indication of where she might have gone or why. It had been a sensation, and not only in the Fox River paper. Both Chicago papers had provided their readers with detailed stories on the mysterious disappearance. Maps of the Grice home had been run by one paper, prompting the other to come up with an aerial photograph of the posh section of Fox River, with the extended riverside Grice property. It did not seem an exaggeration to call it an estate; how may houses sit on three and a half acres overlooking the Fox River?

AG to FG. *Con Amore.*

The abject husband of the missing woman was Arthur Grice. In desperation he had offered ten thousand dollars for any information about his wife.

These events made the inscription in Aggie's ring more than intriguing. Roger Dowling resolved to speak with Aggie about it in the morning.

Two

Mrs. Loring had a long and narrow face that was not helped by the way she wore her hair, brushed back tightly on her head. Her expression was that of a person whose hair was being pulled, which summed up the way she was reacting to the new lease on life her father had taken since being moved from the hospital to the nursing home. His cancer was in remission, not an uncommon thing, but Roger Dowling had been assured by Nagel, the doctor, that this did not alter the grim prognosis. Willis Wirth was unlikely to see another spring. If Audrey Loring had been told this, she apparently did not believe it. Indeed, if she were male and full of darts, she might have been St. Sebastian, though Roger Dowling doubted that she would consider any martyrdom adequate precedent to her own.

"He asked to see you, Father," she said in tones that invited complicity. "He wouldn't take no for an answer."

"How is he?"

"Strong as a horse."

"It was wise to bring him here."

She looked at him blankly, turned and led the way down the hall to the comfortable room in which Willis Wirth awaited his final hour. His hair was gone, his teeth were out, his glasses were so thick they distorted the profile of his face, and he was deaf.

"Anything I had that worked they took out, Father."

When Roger Dowling came within range of Willis Wirth's feeble vision, the old man broke into a gummy smile and began to grope on the bedside table for his teeth. Roger Dowling turned away, lest the old man be embarrassed, but Willis had outlived the slavish concern for the opinion of others. He put his hearing aids in too, one in each ear, and turned them up so high they whistled. Mrs. Loring looked at her father with genuine pity and Roger Dowling realized how little sympathy he had expressed for the daughter. It could not be an easy matter to watch a parent disintegrate before one's eyes. He whispered to her, "He looks good."

"He looks dead," she whispered back and left the room.

"I wasn't sure she called you," the old man shouted. "She thinks I'm a nut, wanting a priest all the time. I would have thought the same thing when I was still a heretic."

Willis Wirth relished describing his previous Unitarian faith in this way. As a convert, he seemed to have accepted everything about Catholicism but the ecumenical spirit.

"But Audrey is a Catholic, Willis."

"By marriage," he said dismissively. He meant that Audrey had come into the Church when she'd married Paul Loring. Willis looked around, annoyed. "Do you hear that noise?"

"I think it may be your hearing aids."

His reaction lacked only a bulb lighting above his head. He stuck his index fingers into his ears and twisted them. He might have been committing suicide.

"Did I call you away from something important?"

It would have sounded unctuous to say that nothing was

more important than ministering to the souls of his parishioners. "We had a magic show tonight at the parish center."

"I never cared for magic."

"The magician was a priest."

"Like Aaron." Willis Wirth had an inexhaustible fund of biblical references. That alone would have marked him as a convert to Catholicism. The cradle Catholic picked up such knowledge as he had of Scripture from the liturgy. "I've been thinking about the Trinity."

The old man had developed a passion for theological discussion and liked nothing better than to spend an hour or more discussing the arcane lore to which he had newly given his assent. Roger Dowling was somewhat less enthused about these amateur forays. More than once he had suggested to Willis that he would be better off praying to God than trying to comprehend him. In any case, it would not be long before all Willis's questions received the only satisfactory answer.

Father Dowling pulled a chair up beside the bed, puffed on his unlit pipe and talked to the dying man of nature and person and relation and the other technical matters theologians had devised to express the incomprehensible mystery. Willis listened intently, breathing rapidly and openmouthed, often closing his eyes. There were stretches when the priest was sure the old man had fallen asleep, but whenever he eased back his chair, the two eyes snapped open and fixed on him.

"Just say when you have to go, Father."

"I don't want to tire you."

"I could listen to you by the hour."

"I'm afraid you have. We'll have another talk soon. It must be consoling to have Audrey and her husband stop by as often as they do."

"She'll be glad when I'm dead." He spoke matter-of-factly and without self-pity. "I don't blame her. From my point of view, I thank God my mind hasn't gone."

"That is a blessing."

"Up to a point. There are days when I envy the gaga vegetables around here."

"You seem to be in fine fettle."

"Nothing has changed, but I'm grateful for the respite."

The old man asked for a blessing and Father Dowling traced the cross over him. Willis Wirth, his theological passion assuaged, and properly blessed, plucked the hearing aids from his ears and let his upper plate hang over his lower lip. He pushed the teeth back in and grinned. "I could put on quite a show myself, Father, but I suspect your audience wouldn't be much better off than I am."

Audrey Loring still sat in the waiting room, smoking a cigarette. Roger Dowling sat down and lit his pipe.

"I thought you'd gone."

She smiled sadly. "Every time I come here I wonder if it will be the last. Do you know, Father, I think I am actually going to miss this place when it's all over."

"That may not be long."

She nodded, after giving it some thought. "I know. I guess I don't really believe it." She leaned forward and put out her cigarette. "I'm still here because Paul is coming for me."

"I could give you a ride."

"He's already on his way. Thank you. I wish I'd thought of that. Paul doesn't like driving in this weather."

Only a dim table lamp illumined the waiting room, and they could easily make out the snowy world outside the windows. The wind swept falling snow across the already covered grounds. The waiting room seemed all the cozier by contrast.

"Dad was angry when I came into the Church. Now he can't talk of anything else."

"That's not unusual with converts."

"I wasn't like that."

He said nothing. As far as he knew, neither she nor Paul were frequent attenders at St. Hilary's. In such places as this, the waiting room, and at such times as this, things were said that might not be in ordinary settings. Roger Dowling smoked quietly, and thought again that he had not felt much sympathy for the Lorings' ordeal.

"Sometimes I think Paul is less of a Catholic than I am."

"Oh?"

"Not that either one of us is much of one, compared with my father."

"It's wise not to get too far away from God."

"Isn't he everywhere?"

"We have to let him in."

She lit another cigarette and put package and lighter back into her purse before blowing smoke at the shadowy ceiling.

"I've taken my cue from Paul. You should talk to him."

Best to let that go. If Paul Loring wanted to talk, he would, and if he didn't, pressure from his wife would not help. Meanwhile, he told Audrey of the magic show at the parish center. Should he mention the ring and its inscription? He did. Audrey did not make the connection he had. Instead she looked at him strangely, as if wondering at this detailed account.

When Paul Loring did show up, stamping snow from his feet and glowering from under thick brows, Roger Dowling felt, as he had before, that Paul Loring found his presence uncomfortable. Paul helped Audrey into her fur, and Roger Dowling, still seated, thought what an odd pair the Lorings made. She was short and thin while he was a great bear of a man, his size almost menacing. The founder and sole proprietor of Loring Construction had an outdoor look, and it was easy to imagine him on building sites. Roger Dowling knew from his own father's experience how iffy it could be to finish a job within the bid that had won it. Paul Loring did not look as though he would be patient with anyone who jeopardized his margin of profit.

"Visiting the sick, Father?" Paul asked with forced cheerfulness.

"Dad insisted I call Father Dowling."

Loring nodded as if conceding a point. "I hope I'm as lucky getting a priest when I die."

But his tone did not suggest that he could really imagine himself seriously ill, let alone dying.

Three

Next morning Roger Dowling looked out at a world whose contours were blurred with snow. It lay in drifts upon the parish lawn, and the roof of the church was thick with it, but the walks that connected rectory, church, and school had already been shoveled—a straight and narrow passage taken down to the concrete. Good old Forbes. Forbes had spent most of his adult life in the merchant marine, and although he had been everywhere, seemed to have seen nothing. Italy for him was Naples and Leghorn, largely dockside.

"And misbehaving, Father," Forbes had said when he'd first showed up at St. Hilary's, looking the priest in the eye. He did not want Roger Dowling to think he had visited the fleshpots of the world for nothing. Now he was in his late sixties and ready to bring his life into line with his beliefs. He had become a regular at the St. Hilary parish center, but his idea of fun was physical labor. He had appointed himself shoveler of sidewalks since the first snow.

"We could get a snowblower," the pastor suggested.

"Not for me, Father. You get one of those and Marie Murkin could clean the walks."

He had raised his voice so the housekeeper could hear, and Marie looked out of her kitchen.

"I don't do windows or shovel snow."

Marie was intimidated by the size of Forbes and by his exaggerated masculinity, but she was a little snobby with him. A lifetime in the rectory had been a liberal education for Marie. St. Hilary parish in Fox River had been her seven seas, and she may well have acquired more knowledge of people there than Forbes had picked up traversing the globe. He, on the other hand, did not seem to know quite how to deal with respectable women.

"I get out of the house as much as I can," he said, referring to the son with whom he lived. "I'm still liable to swear without realizing it and I know it shocks them."

Returning to civilian life was in large part learning a new language, and Forbes was making every effort.

"I see Forbes has already done the walks," Father Dowling said when he came downstairs this morning.

"There won't be many of the old people coming to the center today."

"You may be right."

"May! Look at that snow."

But Marie underestimated the attraction of the parish center for the older parishioners. Besides, weather like this made it an adventure as well. When Roger Dowling went over to the school, Edna told him there were two dozen already there.

"And they keep coming."

Edna Hospers was the main reason for the success of the center. Her husband, Gene, was serving a sentence at Joliet and Edna was raising the children alone. Not only did the job enable her to do that, it distracted her from the loneliness of her life. Moreover, her troubles made her sympathetic with those whose only complaint was growing old.

"The magic show went off well, didn't it, Edna?"

"I think it's half the reason so many are back this morning, Father."

"Is Aggie Miller here?"

"I don't think so. Unless she came in when I didn't notice."

Edna said this without conviction. Aggie Miller never entered or left a room without fanfare. But they went down to the converted gym, where games of checkers, bridge, and shuffleboard were in progress. Forbes stood just inside the door, arms folded, cheeks rosy.

"Father, it's like a cruise ship here. Makes me feel at home."

"I'd love to take a cruise," Edna said.

"Not the way I did," Forbes assured her. "Not much shuffleboard going on in the engine room."

Roger Dowling had taken a silent roll call without seeing Aggie Miller. Well, with this weather, that was hardly a surprise. He buttoned his coat in preparation for the walk back to the rectory. It was strange how the inscription in that ring stayed in his mind. AG to FG. *Con amore.*

Phil Keegan, his car equipped with snow tires, came to the noon Mass and then along to the rectory for lunch; Marie served them chili.

"I thought something hot would be good for a cold day."

"Cold! It's wonderful out, Marie. You ought to get outside yourself. Have you ever thought of taking up cross-country skiing?"

Marie just stared at Phil, uncertain whether or not he was serious. When she spoke it was with a blank expression.

"I think I'll stay with parachute jumping, Captain Keegan."

"Happy landings!" cried a delighted Phil.

He lost some of his exuberance when Roger Dowling asked

him if there was anything new on the disappearance of Frances Grice.

"So you saw the story?"

"What story?"

"This morning's *Tribune*," Marie called from the kitchen. She looked around the doorway. "I have it in here."

The momentary annoyance he felt was insincere. Roger Dowling really had no interest in keeping up with the news, whether in print or on television. The frantic evanescent chatter cluttered the mind with trivia. He much preferred to concern himself with the activities of his parish and to fill his mind from the books on the shelves of his study, particularly with Dante and Aquinas. Let Marie have the newspaper, he really didn't care, although both the *Tribune* and the Fox River paper arrived daily at the door.

"Tell me about it," he urged Phil.

"The newspaper story or the facts?"

"Aha."

They adjourned to the study, where Phil groused about the newspaper criticism of the suburban police force that had been unable after weeks to come up with any leads in the disappearance of the wife of a prominent Fox River developer. According to Phil the story was simply a rehash of the facts, known for months and already featured in previous stories.

"They call it investigative reporting," Phil growled. "Do you know what that means?"

It meant, so far as Phil Keegan was concerned, the printing of any foolish remark a neighbor could be induced to make under questioning by a reporter.

"For all we know, she's sunning herself in Acapulco."

"Are you serious?"

"About Acapulco, no. We checked there because the Grices had vacationed there several times. Grice admits she could just have gone off."

Admits was the operative word, and Phil in turn would have admitted that the theory that Frances Grice had run away to hide was farfetched.

"Is the investigation stopped?"

"Cy Horvath would pursue it even without orders, Roger. Do you really want to talk about this?"

"Not if you don't."

Phil lowered his lids and looked at his old friend.

"Okay. At least this is one case that has nothing to do with St. Hilary's."

Arthur Grice was responsible for some of the most expensive housing that had sprung up in the western suburbs as Chicago continued its crawling westward expansion. Sleepy little towns had been engulfed by developments as national firms built large complexes and their well-paid employees flooded in. They said they were relocating in Chicago, but this really meant some point miles away from the city. Those who worked for the firms had the advantage of a large city's proximity, and for their families a pleasant, previously unspoiled countryside. Natives were understandably less enthused about the dramatic change in their environment, although some, like Arthur Grice, became rich providing new homes, office buildings, schools, and churches. Arthur's father had been a plumbing contractor of moderate success. When Arthur graduated in mechanical engineering from Purdue, he had the intelligence to see what was about to happen to his native region, surprised those who were aware of his ambition by taking over the modest family business, and within five years had borrowed more money than he himself would have dreamed possible when he began.

Wealth is sometimes an elusive thing to identify, particularly with an imaginative entrepreneur like Arthur Grice. Newspaper accounts spoke in reverent tones of his ability to orchestrate a thousand details, bring together need, opportunity, and capital, keeping the overall planning in his own hands. His worth was estimated in the dozens of millions of dollars.

"He's owed more than he owes," Phil Keegan explained. "That seems to be the nature of it. It isn't as if he had all those millions in a bank somewhere. I tell you, Roger, money turns out to be pieces of paper."

"Except for change."

In early September, The Sunday *Tribune* had featured Arthur Grice. His was unequivocally a story of success. Who could have known what tragedy awaited him just around a corner of time?

On September 25, Arthur Grice reported that his wife, Frances, was missing. A tall woman, described as willowy, with platinum-colored hair to the shoulders, and large, serene eyes, she had gazed out at newspaper readers in the early September story, the quintessence of the fashionable and acquisitive class. She had willingly shown reporter and photographer around the estate she and her husband occupied with their horses and dogs and half a dozen cats. No children. No explanation of that, simply no children. Of course, in her mid-thirties, child-bearing was not yet out of the question for Mrs. Arthur Grice, but if any such plans existed they were not revealed to the press. Noteworthy, perhaps, since she and her husband seemed willing to reveal so much else about themselves.

"He is my best friend as well as my lover," she confided to the reporter. "I can't imagine life without him."

He in turn asserted that he never made a business move without a lengthy discussion with Frankie, as he called his wife.

Marie Murkin had kept the original feature as part of her unofficial archives. "He was raised Catholic," she told Father Dowling. "I haven't seen him in church for years. Not since his mother died."

Since Mrs. Grice was active in Planned Parenthood, it was clear she was not Catholic; clear, at least, to Marie. "I hope you're right," Father Dowling said.

A photograph of the Grices astride their matching palominos seemed to sum up the object of suburban longing.

"Marie says Arthur Grice used to attend St. Hilary's," Roger Dowling said to Phil Keegan.

"The Grices belonged to the parish, the mother and father. Nowadays Arthur Grice's religion is money. Maybe that's the source of his trouble."

"But it's not a kidnapping, is it?"

"The wife is not his only problem."

The chink in the Grice armor was Pamela Mathers, the administrative director of Grice Enterprises.

"What is an administrative director?"

"Read this morning's *Tribune.*"

"You were going to save me the trouble."

The story that morning had almost gone beyond innuendo in suggesting that Frankie Grice's disappearance could be explained by the close relationship between Arthur and Pamela. Of course, the point was made by quoting unnamed sources. Phil had Marie bring in the paper, and, folding it over, he handed it to Roger Dowling. Pamela Mathers was a young woman, round-faced, with a scrubbed, boyish look. Jeans tucked into knee-high boots, she was looking at a point upward and to the left of the camera. The photo had been taken on the site of the new civic center that Grice Development was building in the town of Barrington.

"She's cute," Marie said, looking over his shoulder.

It seemed the right word. If Frankie was regal and patrician, Pamela looked like what used to be called a tomboy.

"She doesn't fool the *Tribune,*" Phil said.

Roger Dowling read the story. What in the name of God had happened to a sense of privacy, or for that matter of shame? Subscribers to the *Chicago Tribune* were informed that Pamela Mathers had shared her apartment with a succession of live-in lovers until quite recently, when she had been promoted to executive director at Grice. The man standing behind the young woman was Arthur Grice. The reporter did not actually say that Pamela, having evicted her lover, was available to Arthur Grice, whose lovely wife had obligingly departed the scene. The implication was there, though, along with the darker suggestion that Arthur Grice knew a good deal more of his wife's disappearance than he admitted.

"He should sue for libel," the priest observed, putting down the paper.

"I don't think he will, Roger."

"You think there is something to it?"

"Cy has come up with very damaging information. In the sense that it looks as if Grice *has* been fooling around with Pamela Mathers. Not that he could be indicted for it, but it does make one notice how convenient his wife's disappearance is."

"You think he means to marry Pamela?"

"She's not the marrying kind," Marie Murkin said, and went back to her kitchen.

Phil bundled up and went out to his car, and Roger Dowling was left in his study half wishing he had told Phil of the ring Mrs. Miller had produced at the magic show the night before. He decided to give Aggie Miller a call.

The phone rang several times, but just as Roger Dowling was about to give up the voice of Aggie Miller shouted hello at him.

"Aggie, this is Father Dowling. I noticed you weren't at the center today and called to see if everything is all right."

"How nice of you, Father," she shouted, as if lung power alone could get her voice across the intervening distance.

"You got home all right last night?"

"Oh yes. But I certainly don't intend to leave the house to-day."

"It was a pleasant night, wasn't it, with the magic show?"

"I don't know how that man does it."

"Magicians have always fooled me. I thought he had smashed your ring to bits."

"Well, it wouldn't have been that much of a loss."

"Oh?"

"It's valuable enough but it has no sentimental value for me. I've only had it a month or so."

"Is that right?"

"I bought it at a garage sale. You heard the inscription? I hadn't even noticed there was one when I bought it. In fact, when he read it out last night, it came as news to me, even though I knew it was my ring. The thing is, at the sale I slipped it on and couldn't get it off, and that's why I bought it. I almost never take it off, and then I use lotion. My finger is still sore from twisting it off last night."

"Where was the garage sale?"

"Where?"

"In Fox River?"

"I see what you mean. No. It was in Elgin. I was visiting my daughter and we were driving around. Barb cannot resist a sale of any kind, but garage sales are a must. Well, this was a *street* sale! Anyway, I tried on the ring, couldn't get it off and had to buy it. Not that I regret it. Barbara would have bought if I hadn't. She even tried to buy it from me. I told her she could inherit it along with the rest of my costume jewelry."

He listened to her for fifteen minutes, content to let the old woman's monologue flow freely. Clearly it had not occurred to her whose initials might be inscribed in the ring. After he hung up, he sat for a moment, thinking. Then he picked up the phone again and dialed Phil Keegan.

Four

Even with snow tires, Phil Keegan had a hell of a time getting back downtown from St. Hilary's. The problem was as much his state of mind as the weather. That *Tribune* story, plus recounting the Grice business to Roger, filled him with more frustration than the slippery streets. A thaw the previous afternoon had produced a slick undercoat for the newly fallen snow, and cars were sliding into intersections, horns blaring, drivers unwisely slamming on brakes and spinning as a result. Keegan could have enjoyed the drive, taking the weather on its own terms. The swirling snow and treacherous streets brought back his boyhood, when one went deliberately into a spin on icy streets.

Chief Robertson's solution to the problem was to insist that Frances Grice was a missing person, and they were proceeding to locate her in the established, routine manner. Notice had been sent to major police departments around the country, with an emphasis on areas Mrs. Grice had been known to visit.

The same procedure was being followed with selected places outside the country.

"Maybe we could put her picture on milk cartons," Phil suggested, and for a crazy moment thought the chief would think he was serious.

"Publicity is our best weapon," Robertson admitted primly.

"Well, if it is, the *Tribune* has done us a favor."

"They have, Captain," Robertson said. "Criticism? It's part of the territory. We can take that. But they've put the woman back in people's awareness, and that might help. She could be wandering around Chicago not knowing who she is."

Keegan refrained from commenting that he had seen that movie, too. Their problem wasn't lack of publicity, it was lack of firm evidence to arrest Arthur Grice. Robertson would rather lose half the population than arrest someone like Arthur Grice. Nor would he concede that the *Tribune* piece also drew the obvious conclusion.

"Obvious? What's obvious? The same newspaper was telling us just before the disappearance what a happy couple the Grices were. And they were. Are. I know them, Captain, and no one will ever convince me that Arthur Grice would lift a hand to harm his wife."

Keegan might have applauded this defense of matrimony if he did not think it was motivated by craven fear of offending an extremely wealthy and influential man. Not that Arthur Grice was an easy guy to figure out. There were all kinds of reasons to think that he was devoted to his wife. They had married in Lafayette when they were both undergraduates at Purdue. She had been a Golden Girl with the marching band, as well as an honors student in physics. Not only were they two beautiful people, they were two brilliant people, and it was a toss-up which of the two was the smarter. It didn't matter. They were a team. She had been all for Arthur's returning to Fox River and assuming control of his father's plumbing contracting business. You didn't need an engineering degree from Purdue to be a plumber; on the other hand, not many men became president of a company at the age of twenty-two. Neither one of them thought of it as a plumbing contracting company, period.

What they had seen was possibility, and within a few years some of that possibility was realized. Grice bid on whole jobs, not just the plumbing contract. He put together a consortium of doctors and dentists, and built a private medical facility before they became commonplace. When the doctors realized this was not just a tax shelter but a money-making proposition, he had a fan club whose recommendations led to other clinics. From then on, Grice Enterprises traced a steadily rising line of expansion.

It never went public. Individual projects might involve consortiums and investors, but the parent company, after old Mrs. Grice's death, was wholly owned by Arthur and Frankie Grice.

The point was that the Grices were what Frankie had said they were, friends, not just husband and wife, and even if she seemed to suggest that being friends was more important, it didn't fit in with the notion that her husband would try to get rid of her. Or that she would desert him. Which left them with Robertson's dumb idea that she was wandering around with amnesia, unaware of who she was.

Every other day, Keegan got a call from Grice asking for news about his wife. Keegan shook his head. Things would be very simple if it weren't for Pamela Mathers.

Cy was the soul of discretion, and did not have a habit of seeing what was not there. He was convinced there was something going on between Grice and his administrative director.

"He has stayed overnight at her place several times."

"You're sure?"

Cy nodded. "Those times we know about because of our own surveillance. The stories that he was doing the same thing before his wife disappeared, we accept, if we do, on say-so. Still, it would be hard to discredit the stories."

Could a loving husband be unfaithful? Keegan glared at himself in the rearview mirror. What the hell, it wasn't a question of metaphysics. Anyone could do anything. It was something he and Roger agreed on absolutely. This person might at a given moment be closer to doing something or other than that person, but take away the time factor and they were equally capable. Which meant anyone could be a saint or a son of a bitch. Of *course* Arthur Grice could at one and the same time love his wife and betray her.

When he got to his office he was told that Roger Dowling would like him to call.

"When did he phone?"

Phoebe checked. "An hour ago?"

It must have been shortly after he left. No, that drive from St. Hilary's had taken one long time. He dialed the rectory, and Marie answered.

"Captain Keegan returning Father Dowling's call."

"Mrs. Murkin answering Captain Keegan's call."

"Is he there?"

"Mrs. Murkin will check and see."

"Marie . . ."

But she had let go of the phone and it banged twice against the wall. What a touchy woman, always on her dignity, quick to feel slighted. So why was he grinning?

Five

Drivers did things in snowy conditions they would not ordinarily do, swinging onto busy streets without pausing and to hell with the traffic, they didn't want to take a chance on stopping and having to get going again on a slippery surface. Cy Horvath always drove defensively. Police work had led him to think that on the road, as elsewhere, most people were going to do screwy things, and it was best to be ready for them. So he managed not to get sideswiped when Pamela Mathers sent her Cherokee four-drive into a slide on the Mannheim Road. It wasn't her fault. Some idiot with zero visibility, all his windows covered with snow, swung into her lane without warning. Cy had to hand it to her, the way she handled the jeep, even though she did end up off the road and pointing the wrong way. He eased onto the berm, got out of his car and walked back to her. She sat openmouthed behind the wheel of the vehicle.

"Did you see what that moron did?"

"Police," he said. "Lieutenant Horvath." He opened and closed his identification.

"Police! Why aren't you arresting the ass that ran me off the road?"

"I wanted to make sure you weren't injured."

She decided it was dumb to take her anger out on someone who had stopped because of concern for her.

"I'm all right."

"I'll help you get it turned around."

He gingerly entered the outermost lane and directed cars away from the side of the road while she backed and advanced and finally got the jeep facing the right way.

She rolled down her window before joining the traffic. She had a nice crooked grin. She belonged on the cover of old *Saturday Evening Posts*. "Thanks!" She started to roll up the window, then stopped and peered at him. "Haven't I seen you somewhere?"

"I'm in the Fox River police department. This isn't my jurisdiction."

"So that's why you didn't pull the guy over. Thanks again."

He got back into his car, and within a minute picked up the jeep again, its high center of gravity making it visible over the line of traffic. He felt a lot better tailing her, now that he had spoken with her. But speaking with her, seeing her up close, made what he had learned about her all the harder to believe.

The maintenance man in her building had been willing, even eager, to tell Cy what kind of life Pamela Mathers led.

"They call it lifestyle now as if that made it all right. She has had two different men living with her since she took the apartment."

"She pay the rent?"

Conway nodded twice, bringing his narrow chin down to his protruding chestbone. He reminded Cy of one of those perpetual-motion birds that keeps dipping its beak in water. The maintenance man's quarters were warm and snug, not far from the boiler, a little room festooned with girlie pictures. How much of Conway's story about Pamela Mathers was influenced by an imagination inflamed by soft porn? The man was sixty, maybe more, his skin the same color as his neatly ironed denim overalls, or maybe it just reflected them.

"Sergeant, the whole goddamn world has changed."

"Lieutenant."

"Right. I was an enlisted man." That suggested another line of thought, but he kept to the topic at hand. "The way it is, women are now the way guys have always been."

"How do you mean?"

"Look, a man is out for all he can get, right? He may not cat around but if he gets a chance with some woman he is going to take it. No one would expect him to turn it down."

"And things have changed?"

"Not with men. But before, the chances were few and far between because women more often than not said no. Not any more, Captain. Now they say yes. And if no man asks them, they ask him." Conway had warmed to his subject. His shoulders were still flat against the back of the chair he sat in, but his face had come closer, extended on his thin neck.

"I was born too soon, Lieutenant."

"You're still alive."

"Ha." He drew back his head and laid a finger on his upper lip. "Then again, maybe you're right."

"That you're alive?"

"Look at me, will you? I am an old man. But do you know, there are times when I think they're looking *me* over."

The pictures on the wall looked him over, certainly. Conway's handkerchief had been ironed, too. He did not unfold it when he patted his mouth with it.

"Even Miz Mathers. That's how she says it. Miz."

"Miss Mathers has looked you over?"

Hearing someone else say it aloud seemed to make Conway

realize how ridiculous it sounded. Pamela Mathers could be his granddaughter. Whatever she was doing, Cy wondered if it was any worse than Conway sitting in his overheated office, surrounded by bosomy girls wearing expressions of abandonment, daydreaming about the women tenants.

"Men stayed with Miss Mathers?"

"They lived with her. One at a time, of course." He shook his head. "Why do I say of course?"

"If she paid the rent, you wouldn't know their names."

"I don't collect the rents," Conway said. He seemed unsure whether to be indignant or flattered by the suggestion that he did.

"So you don't know who the men were."

"The first was named Evans. The second was named Stoltman."

"You're sure?"

"Unless they stole the cars they were driving."

"You checked the registration?"

Conway closed one eye and looked wise. "Now it's a guy named Grice. I didn't have to check his car. I seen his picture in the paper. Say." He had both eyes open now and he did not look wise. "Fox River. That's the connection, isn't it? That's where he's from."

"Connection?"

"Why you're interested. What do you think he did with his wife?"

"You got any ideas?"

"I think the two of them got rid of the wife."

"You're just guessing?"

"You asked me if I had any ideas. That's what I think. Take it or leave it."

Cy might not be able to just leave the idea, but he could leave Conway. He felt unclean talking to the maintenance man, as if he too were lurking in a basement near the furnace room spying on tenants and fantasizing about the females.

The fact was that Cy Horvath was as incredulous as Conway about the supposed behavior of youngsters nowadays. He had only a few categories for women as women. They were wives, prostitutes, nuns, or relatives. Prostitutes? Okay. Each one had a story on how she had gotten into the life, but Cy had never met a prostitute who thought the way she made a living was right. He had as much trouble as Conway in imagining a cold-blooded promiscuous woman. Out to get it the way a man was. Jeez, he even sounded like Conway.

That had been three weeks ago. He had been tailing Pamela Mathers pretty much nonstop for a week. Whether or not anything had been going on between Arthur and Pamela before the disappearance of Frances, something was going on now. Some nights he stayed with her. Cy had no difficulty disliking Grice or, at a distance, Pamela. But after her spinout, after helping her get back on the Mannheim Road, after seeing her close up, he just could not believe that fresh-faced, clean-cut, outdoor type could be doing what he knew she had to be doing.

It was still another level of difficulty to imagine that she and Arthur had gotten rid of Mrs. Grice. Not to mention the practical impossibility of providing a prosecutor with evidence that incriminated someone in the disappearance of someone else. They did not know whether anything had been done to Frances Grice, let alone whether she had been killed. Add to that mix the fact that Arthur Grice got furious at any suggestion that his wife would not be found.

"I don't want any excuses for not looking for her."

This was addressed to Robertson, so both Phil Keegan and Cy kept quiet.

"Our search continues," the chief said obsequiously. "But we do have limited resources, Mr. Grice, even if finding your wife was the only thing confronting us."

The next day Grice announced he was hiring a private detective and increasing the reward to fifty thousand dollars for information leading to the discovery of his wife.

"Dead or alive?" Keegan asked. The captain had just put out one of his cigars. Cy objected less to the smell of them lit than put out.

"It doesn't say."

"Fifty thousand dollars," Keegan said in wondering tones. "Agonized husband desperate for the return of his wife." He was suggesting the tone of the press coverage.

"For the first time I think he did it."

"The reward's a smoke screen?"

"And he hired Horowitz."

Keegan laughed. The mention of Horowitz's name had that effect in the department. Duke Horowitz had dreamed of becoming a cop since he was a kid, but at five feet, two inches, he simply couldn't qualify even if he had been a lot smarter. Turned down by every police department in the Chicago area, he had gone farther afield but met with disappointment wherever he applied. During this fruitless quest, he worked in a supermarket, first as bag boy, then checker, and finally assistant manager. His ambition was assuaged somewhat by the pursuit of shoplifters, but it hadn't been enough. And then one day, to everyone's surprise, he set himself up as a private investigator. He had taken a correspondence course, been granted a licence, and he was now a certified and licenced private investigator.

He rented offices in a building that city planning had targeted for destruction but had never been able to bring down because a small, dedicated group of preservationists, who professed to see the hand of the Sullivan school in the building's facade, always managed a last-minute reprieve. A license, an office, a telephone, an ad in the yellow pages—Horowitz had everything but clients. By and large, he was reduced to security work. For Horowitz to be hired by Arthur Grice to find his missing wife was to the police a sick joke. But the media, in the shape of Mervel, a Fox River journalist, applauded this effort to circumvent the inept police. The offer of fifty thousand dollars gave the effort its bona fides.

"Maybe he doesn't know about Horowitz?"

"How could he not?" Keegan growled.

What angered Keegan was the explicit criticism of the department involved in Grice's move.

Horowitz drove a former taxi that must have had two-hundred-thousand miles on it. The camouflage coat of paint had faded, and the checkered band was once more visible around its midsection. Horowitz was tailing Pamela Mathers too, but as far as Cy could see Duke always lost her before she went a mile. In any case, while the ex-cab was in on it from the beginning, it always dropped out soon after. But whenever Pamela got back to Grice Enterprises, there was Horowitz, parked in a visitor's spot, waiting. The big question was, if Horowitz had been hired by Arthur Grice to find his wife, what was he doing following Pamela Mathers?

"You asking me to break the confidence of a client?"

"No, just to answer a simple question. Why are you following Pamela Mathers?"

"I can't answer that question." *Spartan* was the word that came to mind at the sight of Duke Horowitz's office. The furniture consisted of a trestle table available at discount houses for maybe twenty dollars, two folding chairs, a three-drawer file cabinet, wooden, that looked like army surplus and a veteran of Bataan. The surprising item was the personal computer set up on the table. Duke sat in front of it, hands poised over the keyboard as if he were the other Horowitz.

"Okay. I'll pass it on to Mervel. His readers know you were hired to find Grice's wife. Let him speculate why you are tailing his girlfriend."

Horowitz's hair was thick and black on the sides and gone on top. He lay one hand on his head like a yarmulke.

"You wouldn't do that?"

"You opposed to freedom of the press?"

"I'll tell you why I'm following her."

"I thought you might."

"Grice told me to. He's worried the ones who got his wife will get her. She thinks she's being followed."

"She is."

Horowitz moved the hand from his head to the desk. "By who?"

"By you."

Horowitz swore as if he were repeating a lesson in a foreign language.

Cy said, "What have you reported to Grice?"

"Nothing in writing. I talked to him last night."

"And?"

"I told him not to worry."

"What did he say?"

"Stay on it."

When Cy told Keegan this, the captain would think Grice was jealous of Pamela and suspected her of seeing someone else. The perils of promiscuity. It made sense. Unless Grice had sized Horowitz up, thought he was good for publicity purposes, and was letting him waste his time trying to follow Pamela around town. What Cy did not like was the possibility that Pamela had noticed him following her.

So today he had faced her, and she said he looked familiar, and that could mean anything.

On the way down the hall after leaving Duke Horowitz, he knocked sharply on Tuttle's closed door, and then ducked into the stairway and went down to his car on foot.

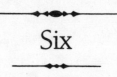

Six

Tuttle, his Irish tweed hat pulled low over his eyes, looked out of his office door, first to the right, then to the left, ducked back in, and a moment later looked out again, his head emerging at a different level than before.

He closed the door, waited, and after half a minute pulled the door quickly open and rushed into the hallway. Empty. Hands on hips, he looked toward the stairway, pivoted and looked at the glow coming through the frosted glass of Horowitz's door. Was the new tenant a comedian?

On his own door was the somewhat puzzling legend, Tuttle & Tuttle, Attorney at Law. The second Tuttle was his father, whose sacrifices had sent him through law school, and who had earned in gratitude this posthumous partnership. Inside again, Tuttle went through the empty outer office—he had given his secretary leave of absence during this slack period— and went on into an eight-by-eight room, one wall of which was law books as dusty as the windows. But Tuttle was indifferent to his surroundings. He sat behind the desk, put his feet up on the desk, tipped his hat low over his eyes, and wondered if he had dreamed that knock on the outer door.

Had he been asleep? The line between sleep and waking was indistinct at this hour of the afternoon on a snowy day in Fox River. A heavy snowfall had the effect of erasing the years and returning him to the carefree outlook of his youth. Not that he had enjoyed much time for play. At ten he had begun to sell morning papers on a street corner, rising before six o'clock to do this, getting to school at nine. At the age of twelve he had a *Tribune* paper route. Summers he caddied or worked at one of the marinas on the Fox River. But winter and snow spelled an undefinable peace for Tuttle; he was not quite sure why.

The pipes began a rhythmic pounding. Whatever faults this building had, it was well heated. Earlier he had sat looking out his window, mesmerized by the falling snow, carried back, back, back to when his father had been alive, his father who had been a one-man cheering squad for Tuttle, encouraging, praising, sacrificing for him. At some point in the daydream, Tuttle adjusted his hat . . .

And slept. But in dreams Tuttle returned to the anxieties of his fitful practice. What he needed was a big break, a bonanza, someone who despite the long run of bad luck would see beneath the surface to the real Tuttle, hire him, and open the way to affluence. Someone like Lowry or Cadbury. Someone like Arthur Grice.

He awoke so suddenly he nearly fell off the chair. Grice! He remembered the knock on the door and his fruitless search of the hallway, and it was all he could do not to fall on his knees and thank God. Of course. It was opportunity knocking. He knew Horowitz had been taken on by Arthur Grice to find his wife, he knew there was a fifty thousand dollar reward, and still he sat here as if his prayers had not been answered.

What did he want, a voice speaking from the heavens? He creaked forward in his chair, put his feet flat on the floor, took off his hat, sailed it toward the coatrack, and scored a ringer!

One more sign that out of the blue on this snowy day, his luck was about to change.

Horowitz. He knew the man was in. He picked up the phone and called information for the number of Duke Horowitz in the Dupont Building.

"That number is in the directory, sir."

"What page?"

"I beg your pardon."

"What's the number, sweetheart?"

"I'll ring it for you."

He lowered his voice. "Can you give it to me first?"

"Sir, I will report you for making an obscene call."

The line went dead. A genuinely puzzled Tuttle got up, went down the hall, and walked into Horowitz's office. Duke was seated at his computer.

"I need you for a job, Horowitz."

The poor devil could not keep delight from his face. "Who are you?"

"Tuttle. Of Tuttle and Tuttle. What are your rates?"

"What's the job?"

Tuttle pulled the door closed and dragged the other folding chair to the table.

"From this point on this is strictly a confidential communication."

Horowitz's eyes widened. The mustache was a mistake, but Tuttle let it go. The detective nodded.

"I want to put a tail on Arthur Grice."

Horowitz hit a key and a succession of sentences began to appear on the screen. "You're kidding."

"I never kid."

"Let me give you a confidential answer. Arthur Grice is my client. It was in the news. Everybody knows."

"That's right," Tuttle said.

"What do you mean, that's right?"

"I say we should join forces."

"I don't understand you."

"Concentrate. We're both after the same thing."

"Are we?"

Tuttle couldn't figure Horowitz. Was he as dumb as he looked? As for Tuttle, he had come down the hall with the sense that he had been sent; one way or the other he was meant to be here. Suddenly it occurred to him that Horowitz had offices in the Dupont Building.

"How much did Grice offer you, Horowitz?"

"That's none of your business."

"You're wrong about that and let me tell you why."

A moment went by. "Go ahead. Tell me."

But Tuttle still waited for inspiration. "How does twenty-five thousand sound to you?"

Horowitz was thoroughly confused. "Are we talking about what Grice offered me?"

"No, Horowitz. Twenty thousand is my offer."

"You said twenty-five."

"It keeps going down until you tell me you're working for me."

"In advance?"

"It's going to go down to fifteen in . . ." He pulled back his sleeve, turning away as he did so. He did not have a wrist watch. Behind him a chair hit the floor. Horowitz had upset it when he'd leapt to his feet. Tuttle smiled. He had an employee.

"What do you want me to do?"

"What have you learned so far?"

"Wait a minute. I want a retainer."

Without a word, Tuttle took out a checkbook, opened it, and boldly wrote a twenty-five thousand dollar check made out to . . . "What's your first name?"

"Nathan."

"Good name." He completed writing the check, tore it out, studied it, then handed it to Horowitz. "You got a safe?"

Horowitz looked around as if there was something in the bare room he hadn't noticed before.

"You want to keep it overnight in my office, that's okay, with me."

Horowitz shook his head and stuffed the check into the inner pocket of his greenish sport coat. The account on which the check was written was closed, but just to be safe Tuttle had written 1888. He would say it had been a joke, and his banker would agree that a twenty-five thousand dollar check from Tuttle & Tuttle was Monopoly money. Not that he meant to cheat Horowitz. He would split the fifty thousand dollar reward with him.

"Okay, report."

"On what?"

"What have you been doing the last few days?"

"Following Pamela Mathers."

"The girlfriend? He had you doing that?"

Horowitz nodded.

Why would Arthur Grice hire Horowitz to find his missing wife and then have him tail Pamela Mathers? This tidbit was almost worth twenty-five thousand. Grice was more worried about Pamela than he was about his wife. Worth thinking about, that.

Horowitz cleared his throat, but he still sounded like a soprano when he spoke. "So what do you want me to do?"

"Come down to my office so we can be comfortable. Don't you want to turn that off?"

"It's best to keep a computer running."

"You're right. Tell me something, Horowitz, was that you knocked on my door earlier?"

"No."

"It didn't sound like you."

Tuttle could almost believe it was his sainted father who had summoned him from the other world and pointed him toward a real bonanza. What he wouldn't give to have a good talk with Dad now. He looked quickly at Horowitz.

"Your parents alive, Nathan?"

"Sure."

"Both of them?"

"Yeah."

"Thank God for it."

"You don't know my parents."

"I'd love to meet them sometime."

Seven

The call from Father Dowling had been a godsend. Even a day later, Aggie Miller awoke in a still-buoyant mood because someone had cared about her enough to call. She had gotten used to living alone, more or less, but the sense of being penned up in the house unnerved her. That was why, despite the storm, she had gone to the magic show at the parish center two nights ago. A magic show! It had turned out to be fun but now, despite that, the thought of going out into a blizzard to watch a grown man, a priest at that, fool others, seemed slightly mad. Just to be where there were people, though, and bright lights, excitement, and chatter, had made it worthwhile.

This was why old people went to malls, she was told, though it was not her practice. To get to a mall without a car was all but impossible. The only mall she knew well was the one in Elgin to which Barbara took her. Once, they had sat on a bench near the indoor waterfall and watched the retired people walk by, wearing sweat suits, caps, and tennis shoes, swinging their arms and trying to remember what it was like to be agile. Aggie disapproved. Aggie thought of herself as, by contrast, growing old gracefully. She couldn't imagine herself bouncing through a mall with rinsed hair and elaborately laced tennis shoes, looking like a beach ball in jogging costume. Living alone bred its own eccentricities, however.

Talking to herself, for instance. She no longer even tried to stop herself from talking aloud while she was alone. What difference did it make? Talk is just thinking out loud, and there was no way she could stop thinking. Sometimes she mimicked conversation, of course, and not only when she talked back to the television. She would get into imaginary conversations with Barbara after a visit or after a phone call, continuing in a one-sided way discussions begun with her daughter. Before Father Dowling called yesterday, she had been talking nonstop.

When she awoke that morning and saw the frost on the windows and, getting up on an elbow, saw the snow still falling, she wanted to curl up in a ball and stay right there in bed. She had the electric blanket turned up to four, which was close to being uncomfortable, but her bed was snug. At least until she began to think of the whole house as closing in on her the way the bedclothes did, the snow a blanket that covered and suffocated as well.

After that she had to get up, but she left her nightie on and slipped into the oversize baby-blue robe Barbara had given her for Christmas. It seemed a promise to herself that she could go back to bed if she wanted to.

While she had talked with Father Dowling, she had prided herself on the tone of her voice, vigorous and loud. She dreaded the thought of people referring to poor old Aggie Miller, all alone in that big house. The impression she wanted to create, and felt she did, was that of a widow who had adjusted to life alone, who was alert and busy and very far indeed from being an object of pity.

But how nice it had been of Father Dowling to call. She

thought this a day later while walking through the house with a cup of tea, unable to settle in any room. She had the television on in the sitting room and she had the radio on in the kitchen, and the sound of voices was reassuring. But the sense of snow enveloping the house and the storm, now in its third day, made her restless. The lower parts of the windows were covered with the most intricate filigrees of frost, and the upper portions of the panes were steamy, so it was impossible to see out. Two weeks earlier, on public television there had been a documentary on Antarctica, and she had been unable to watch it. The thought of being pent up in buildings that disappeared beneath the snow struck her uncomfortably as too much like being buried alive.

Thoughts of the magic show were revived by remembering Father Dowling's call and the trick Father Don had performed with her ring. She held her right hand out before her and looked at the way the flesh of her finger flared out on either side of the ring. She must get it sized. It was much too tight for comfort. Imagine its having an inscription! She had left her glasses in the car when they'd stopped at the street sale, so she hadn't noticed it when she'd bought it. Since then, when she used lotion to remove it—which had only been twice—she wasn't wearing glasses. What had the inscription read?

She went into her bedroom and pressed some lotion into the palm of her left hand, and then began to lubricate the ring finger of her right. Even so, it took an effort to get the ring off. How had she managed it the other night, unaided? But she had offered, so she'd had to remove it, no matter how painful. The lotion was a good idea, if only to work out the soreness. She held the ring up to the light and tipped her head back to look through the lower lens. AG to FG. *Con amore*. What language was that? With love? Wondering whose initials they were, she felt that she was invading the privacy of others. What emotion must have been behind the decision to buy this ring, to have it inscribed, to present it? Aggie's eyes grew moist as she imagined a faceless man looking into her eyes as he slipped the ring onto her finger. She leaned her hip against the basin and lifted her face, eyes closed.

A moment later she shook her head. Catching sight of her flushed face in the mirror, she flushed more deeply with embarrassment. For the love of God. She was sixty-two years old and here she was daydreaming like a girl. She would be shocked to think that her daughter indulged in such reveries, and Barbara was just thirty. She slipped the ring into the pocket of her robe. The next time she went out, she would stop by a jeweler's and have him make it larger. Have him remove the inscription, too.

Tugging her robe tightly about her, she went into the front hallway to see if she could see out from there. But the panes in the door were frosted over. She rubbed away the ice with the heel of her hand and put her face close to the opening. A man was shoveling her walk.

It took a moment for surprise to set in. It was definitely her walk he was clearing, not just the public one. He was working on the steps that came up from the public sidewalk, and even as she watched, he positioned his shovel and began to push it up the walk toward the front door. Snow curled away from the blade and soon rose above and covered it. He stopped and stepped backward, then pushed forward again. If he intended simply to push a path to the door, he found the snow was too deep for that. He could just walk through the snow if all he wanted was to get to the door, but obviously cleaning the walk was his aim. He widened the initial path, pushing snow to right, then left, exposing the walk, then advancing to another section. Who on earth was he?

She had the fleeting thought that he was the man in her daydream in the bathroom, and her hand closed around the ring in her pocket. Silly. She had spoken aloud and her breath caused steam to form on the glass. She rubbed it away. She decided she had never seen the man before. He was all bundled up against the cold, wearing a fingertip coat with a fur collar and a Russian-style fur cap. If he were a delivery man there would have been a truck, but the curbing in front of her house was free of parked cars. He obviously was not a mailman, but maybe he was from one of the package delivery companies. Except that he had no package, only a shovel, and it didn't make much sense to shovel a walk that clean just to get to the door.

He must be doing it by mistake, she decided, that was the only explanation. He wasn't a neighbor, of course, she would recognize a neighbor no matter how bundled up. The decent thing to do would be to open the door and tell him whose house this was. She undid the chain, turned the key in the dead-bolt lock, and gripped the knob in both hands. The weather stripping had come loose jamming the door, and it was almost as hard as getting the ring off her finger to open it.

The storm door pushed outward and the accumulated snow resisted her pushing, but finally she felt the rush of cold air, stuck her face outside and felt the falling snow.

"Helloooo," she called. "Yoohoo."

He continued to shovel—he was halfway up the walk—and she called again. He stopped, straightened and looked toward her.

"This is the Miller residence," she called.

He seemed to wait for her words to get to him. He nodded.

"Why are you shoveling my walk?"

She spoke each word separately, as if she were sailing them like frisbees into the wind. When the man understood what she had said, he smiled, nodded, and set to work again. Puzzled, a little amused, and intrigued, Aggie pulled in her face and closed the storm door. Its window was steaming up rapidly, but she kept it clear so she could watch the shoveler's progress. Until he got to the door, she would not learn who he was and what he was doing.

He got to the steps and then did a particularly thorough job on them. Aggie realized she was grinning in anticipation of his explanation. There was a tap on the storm door and she pushed it out gently. He was standing on the top step, and he looked in at her.

Looked down at her, actually, although he was standing on a step below the threshold. His eyes twinkled with good humor, his face was ruddy with cold and he was breathing heavily.

"Why did you shovel my walk?" she asked and could not repress a giggle.

"Just a courtesy, fair lady."

"Who are you?"

He smiled indulgently. "I heard you correctly when you said this was the Miller residence?"

"Yes it is." Television fantasies. He was Ed McMahon, come to give her ten million dollars. She sent in entries for all such promotional lotteries but without ordering anything, and she was sure her envelope would never even be kept for the drawing. Yet here was Ed McMahon to prove her wrong and make her rich beyond her wildest dreams. "I'm Aggie Miller." This was how she always filled in the coupons.

"Then this is the right house. May I come in?" He leaned his shovel against the house as if there could be no possibility of a denial. And how could she say no after he had cleaned her sidewalk so nicely? She stepped back into house, and he followed, filling up the entryway. He was wearing rubbery boots that he began to stamp. Given his size and the vigor of the stamping, she could imagine his foot disappearing through the floor.

"Would you like something hot to drink?"

"Is that coffee I smell?"

"You will," she said, and went off to the kitchen.

It was undeniably exciting that she had a man in her house. Maybe he would like a full breakfast? She turned to ask and was surprised to find that he had come along with her and was close behind her. She brushed against him as she turned. When she looked up, she was reassured by his smile.

"Have you had breakfast?"

"All I need is coffee, ma'am."

He caught her hand and lifted it in a gesture of gallantry. Would he have kissed it if she hadn't pulled it free and fled into the kitchen? She had the first premonition that she had done something very foolish.

"You're not wearing the ring," he said.

"What ring?"

The smile had gone now, and he moved rapidly toward her, grabbing her wrist painfully and pulling her against him.

"The ring that was used in the magic show."

"Let go of my hand, please."

"Where the hell is that ring?"

She kicked him ineffectually (she was wearing her bunny slippers), and tried to free her wrist. There was no doubt that his mood had changed. What in God's name had she done, letting this monster into her house?

"It's in the bathroom, on the sink."

He looked at her, skepticism draining from his face. "In the bathroom?"

"On the sink. I just took it off."

He examined the hand he held, then nodded. Aggie felt a flood of relief. He would take the ring and go. That is what he had come for. Well, he could have it!

But he did not let go her hand. He tugged open a drawer, shut it, opened another. He had found what he wanted. The blade of the butcher knife catching a glint of sun from the frosted window was the sight she carried with her into eternity.

Eight

Roger Dowling stood in the living room of the Miller house with Phil Keegan, who had just joined him after talking with the medical examiner's people at work in the kitchen.

"Her throat was cut."

"My God."

"Nothing else."

It took a moment before he realized that Phil was referring to rape.

"Robbery?"

"Let's look around."

The bedroom had been torn apart, drawers pulled from the dresser and their contents strewn over the room. A tiered jewelry box lay on its side, necklaces, earrings, bracelets, brooches, and rings cast aside.

"He was looking for something."

"I wonder if he found it."

When Phil had arrived at the Miller house, following up on
Roger Dowling's call the previous afternoon, he had been
struck by the fact that the sidewalk was cleared, recently too,
since the still-falling snow had scarcely covered it again. The
storm door was not tightly closed, and the inner door stood
open. He called into the house, but already had an apprehension of what awaited him.

He found the body in the kitchen, and stepped over it because a cold wind swept through the room from the open back
door. He looked out at the tracks that crossed the lawn to the
fence. There were bushes on the other side of the fence, and
beyond that a house. No sign of anyone. Those tracks, on
closer examination, could have been made hours ago. At first
he had thought his yelling had sent someone running out the
back. It was all he could do to stop himself from taking off
after him, but that would have been stupid. He stepped back
over the body—if she wasn't dead, he would turn in his
badge—and took the phone from the wall. After calling downtown, he phoned Roger Dowling.

"Your telling me yesterday about the inscription in her ring
is why I came here," Phil told the priest after he'd arrived.
Roger Dowling was in the house ten minutes after taking Phil's
call.

"Do you think that's what he was after?"

Phil thought the look of the bedroom made that plausible. If
the thief had been scared off, there was a good chance he had
not found it.

"Wait a minute," Phil said.

He went off to the kitchen, and Roger Dowling did not follow him. He had prayed over Aggie when he'd arrived, giving
her conditional absolution—do we really know when death
comes?—and had no desire to see the bloody scene again. Phil
came back to say she was not wearing any rings but her wed-
ding rings.

"What did the ring look like, Roger?"

"Oh, I'm sure that just about anyone else could describe it better than I could."

"Anyone else?"

"Anyone else who was at the magic show."

But even as he said it, he realized that only those at the magic show could have known of the ring, and more importantly of the inscription inside it.

When they came out of the bedroom, the body was being carried in a rubber bag by two men talking loudly about the Bears, as if to distract themselves. They were carrying from her house Aggie Miller, who perhaps an hour ago had every reason to think many years of life still lay ahead of her.

The deadbolt lock told Phil Aggie had opened the door to her assailant. There was no sign of struggle in the entryway. Indeed, except for the kitchen and the bedroom, the house looked spic and span.

"It could have been just robbery, Roger."

"What did he take?"

"That's not for me to say. She might have had cash in the house, government bonds."

"Jewelry?"

"He could have taken good stuff and left the junk. I wouldn't know. But we will find out."

Roger Dowling was certain it was the ring that explained Aggie Miller's death. The magic show, his telephone call to her yesterday, the fact that he had alerted Phil—all that seemed like a prelude to what had happened to Aggie in the kitchen.

A tall lugubrious-looking man came out of the kitchen. Kite, the assistant coroner.

"You can seal it off now, Captain."

The walkway to the street was now passable, more because of the tramping back and forth than because of the earlier shoveling. Kite picked his way out to his car.

"I wonder who shoveled the walk?" Roger Dowling asked.

"Probably some neighbor kid. I'll have it checked out."

"Can you stop by the rectory, Phil?"

"Later, if I may. I should go downtown first."

When Roger Dowling got back to St. Hilary's, the old people who had spent the day at the parish center were being picked up by daughters or sons. Had they heard about Aggie Miller? Roger did not have it in him to stop and pass on the sad news. He hurried from the garage to the rectory, head down against the snow, glad of the prospect of being inside in weather like this. Marie must have heard his car. The door was open when he reached the porch, and he hurried into the warm kitchen. Marie was dying for news of what had happened to Aggie. Well, he could hardly deny her that.

"A butcher knife?" The housekeeper shuddered and closed her eyes. "The poor woman. God rest her soul."

"Amen to that."

"But why?"

"The police think it was robbery. There wasn't anything else."

Whether or not Marie understood, she certainly would not ask him if Aggie Miller had been raped as well as murdered. And he would only be oblique about it with her.

"What would she have worth the taking, I wonder?"

"Do you want to know my theory?"

"I can guess," Marie said.

"Tell me."

"The magic ring."

"Why do you think so?"

"Was it missing?"

"It seems so. She wasn't wearing it."

"But that means it was Arthur Grice who killed her."

"Except for one thing. There is no way he could have known Aggie had that ring. And none of the people who could have known could possibly have done this."

· 50 ·

He meant the handful of people who had turned out for Don's magic show and heard the inscription read. Aggie herself had not previously known of the inscription. Roger Dowling went on to the study, where he lit a pipe and thought of those who had watched Don's magic show. There seemed to be no menacing member in the group. And would they have told anyone else? Told them what? He himself had, by the sheerest accident, connected the inscription with the Grices. He had no reason to think anyone else had. Aggie certainly did not. But if one or two of the old people had matched the initials with the Grices, whom might they tell who would break in on Aggie Miller? Who could want the ring badly enough to kill for it, except Arthur Grice?

Slow down, slow down, he told himself. He was erecting a house of cards on the flimsiest of foundations. He was assuming that the ring was involved in the death of Aggie Miller. He was assuming that the initials stood for Arthur and Frances Grice. He was assuming that the ring suggested harm or death had come to Frances Grice, and that Arthur Grice, having killed his wife, having heard the ring was in Aggie Miller's possession, convinced this constituted a threat to him, killed her to get it back. And he was assuming that the ring had been stolen from Aggie Miller.

The phone rang and Roger Dowling picked it up, but not before Marie had answered it in the kitchen. Phil was calling.

"I'm on the line," Roger Dowling said.

"The ring was in the pocket of her robe, Roger. So we can rule that out as a motive."

"On what basis?" Marie asked indignantly.

"It wasn't stolen," Phil said.

"You mean it wasn't found. Look how long it took you to find it."

"You still on, Roger?"

"Are you coming over?"

"What's for dinner, Marie?"

"Meat loaf."

"Is that an invitation, Roger?"

Phil would come in an hour. After he hung up, Marie said, "That doesn't prove a thing, Father."

"You may be right."

He felt the same way, but it was unwise to get into the grips of a theory. With a little ingenuity, anything can be made to conform to a theory fiercely enough held.

He was bringing a match to his pipe when it occurred to him that Phil Keegan would have to confront Arthur Grice with the ring and ask him if it had belonged to his wife. The match burned close to his fingers before he blew it out. And what could be done if Grice denied the ring had been his wife's? AG to FG. *Con amore.* With love. There was no way to tell whether it was Italian or Spanish. Or was it *amor* in Spanish? And why would Arthur Grice use either?

When Phil came he listened to the suggestion that he now confront Arthur Grice with the ring, and then held up his hand.

"Whoa. Roger, there is no connection between the murder of Aggie Miller and the disappearance of Frances Grice. There is no reason to think so."

"The inscription in the ring?"

"Look, Aggie Miller said it was bought in Elgin. How many AGs and FGs do you suppose there are in a city the size of Elgin? You don't know, I don't know. But more than enough to make it ridiculous to think this ring was given by Arthur Grice to his wife."

"What harm can asking do?"

Phil turned toward the kitchen door. "Great meat loaf, Marie."

The voice of the housekeeper was heard offstage. "What harm *can* it do, Captain?"

Nine

When Phil Keegan and Cy Horvath called on Arthur Grice with the ring that had been found on the murdered Aggie Miller, they were in possession of several important facts.

First, the ring had been purchased by Arthur Grice some three years earlier from a Fox River jeweler, the fourteenth Agnes Lamb had called on.

Second, Willa Hopkins, Aggie Miller's next-door neighbor, had provided a description of the man who had shoveled Aggie's walk that fateful morning. She had also seen him leave across the backyard, carrying his shovel. The description vaguely fit Arthur Grice, but it would be impossible to go beyond that.

Lionel Dolan was happy to identify himself as the jeweler of Arthur and Frances Grice. "He made it sound like a royal appointment," Agnes said, rolling her eyes. She described him as a short, soft man whose glasses seemed only slightly weaker versions of the magnifying lens attached to their frame.

"He remembered the ring?" Keegan did not want to encourage Agnes's proletarian complaints. Agnes was the first and so far the only black woman on the force, an excellent cop and not the token she had been hired as, and her asides were seldom irrelevant.

"He keeps records. He had a file on the Grices; their parents too. The idea is that the items are all registered. Now, they don't do that at K-Mart."

"So we'll have more trouble finding you," Cy said.

"We haven't found anyone yet," Keegan growled. "How about the inscription?"

"He had that written down, too. You think *con amore* means with love, don't you?"

"What does it mean?"

"With love. But it was also meant to be a kind of anagram on Connemara, which is where her family comes from."

"It doesn't sound like Dolan is confusing this ring with any other."

"No sir."

"How many items were in his Grice file?"

"Lots. Three or four from her to him, at least a dozen items from him to her. A pendant watch, a star sapphire encircled by diamonds, pearls . . ."

As she spoke, Keegan consulted the list of items that had been spilled across Aggie Miller's dresser, but there were no matches.

Keegan decided against taking Agnes along to the corporate offices of Grice Enterprises on the Southwest side of Fox River. Exaggerated eaves carried the low building's slight incline forward in a rakish way, over the windowed wall in which the main entrance was set. A uniformed individual met them inside, with an inquiring look that soon dissolved into consternation.

"Captain Keegan? Cy! What are you doing here?"

Joe Walsh looked afraid that he was going to be called back

on active duty, away from this cushy job presiding over the lobby of the Grice building while drawing the pension he had earned during twenty years on the force.

"We're here to see the big man, Joe. He's expecting us."

"I'll show you the way."

This slowed their progress since Joe Walsh was a little gimpy, with arthritis of the knee. Grice's outer office could have accommodated a tennis court. When Keegan saw the receptionist, he wished he had brought Agnes Lamb along. The woman's dress was of at least eight very bright and basic colors, her hair was cut to an eighth of an inch all over, and her chiseled features suggested Ethiopian origins. The white dots of her earrings accented the smooth, coffee-colored skin.

"Captain Keegan here has an appointment with Mr. Grice," Joe Walsh said, and his was not the voice of authority.

Madeleva, as the sign on her desk identified her, nodded and smiled, revealing two rows of perfect and very large teeth. "He is expecting you, Captain Keegan."

Grice was halfway across his office to the door when they came in. He kept coming, eyes burning into Keegan's.

"What have you found?"

"I don't know how significant it is."

"What is it?"

"A ring. I wonder if you would identify it."

"A ring!" Grice stepped back and looked at Cy and then at Walsh, who had followed them in. Grice's look of disappointment turned to a frown. Walsh mumbled something and left. Meanwhile Keegan went on to the desk, where he took the ring from his handkerchief and held it up to the light before putting it on the desktop. Grice leaned over to peer at the ring, then picked it up.

"I gave this ring to my wife."

"And had it engraved?"

Grice thought a moment, then tilted the ring to the light. "I had forgotten that." He turned to Keegan. "Where did you find it?"

"Was your wife wearing that ring the last time you saw her?"

"She must have been."

"Why?"

"It was her favorite ring. Is this all you found?"

"Yes."

"Is it a lead?"

"I don't know."

Grice moved toward a leather sofa and waved Keegan and Horvath to a matching one that stood at a right angle to it. Keegan said, "Did you read about a woman named Miller who was killed in her home two days ago?"

"Miller? What does she have to do with my wife?"

"This ring was in her possession. In the pocket of the robe she was wearing when she was killed. The house had been ransacked and her throat was cut with a butcher knife. If the thief was looking for the ring, he didn't get it."

Grice followed this account impatiently. "Where did the woman get Frankie's ring?"

"She told people who noticed it that she had bought it at a garage sale in Elgin."

"When?"

"We still can't say. I wanted you to know this as soon as we were sure."

"Sure the ring was Frankie's?"

"A jeweler named Dolan identified it."

"I bought it from him. Tell me, Captain Keegan, where does this ring lead you?" He held it now between thumb and index finger, studying it. Keegan did not think Grice could have got the ring on his little finger.

"All we have is routine, Mr. Grice. We will find where that sale was held in Elgin. We will try to find out where the items sold there came from. Sooner or later, this could take us to your wife."

"Sooner or later." Grice groaned aloud. "Where is she now? That's what I want to know, where is she right now?"

He turned and looked out the window over the snow-covered lawn of his headquarters, an agonized expression on his face. He sat sideways on the couch, one haunch covering two of its four cushions, a powerful man, however dejected.

"You don't know Aggie Miller?"

He shook his head without turning.

"One of the neighbors saw the man who first cleaned her sidewalk and then killed her."

Keegan said nothing more, and in a moment Grice turned away from the window and faced Keegan. "What did he look like?"

"You."

"You're kidding."

"No. It wasn't you, was it?"

More in sorrow than in anger, Grice said, "No, Captain Keegan, I did not kill that woman. In case you read the *Tribune,* I will tell you I did not kill my wife, either." He slapped his extended right-hand palm onto the couch. The sound might have been that of a hand against a face. "And by God I want her found. You've spent months on your routine and it sounds to me as if it was blind chance that you found this ring. Well, let me tell you something, Captain. A week ago I hired a detective named Horowitz as a joke, as a prod. I wanted to do something to make you people realize that you are accomplishing absolutely nothing. Now I mean to bring in a top-notch investigating firm and get some action."

"That's not a bad idea."

"Captain, it's my only hope. I sure as hell can't rely on you."

"We can't put the whole department onto one case."

"One good man could have solved this long ago."

Watching Grice go from calm to angry, from soft to loud, Keegan was unable to form an opinion about the man. Anger is always a good disguise, but Grice had seemed truly moved at the sight of his wife's ring and its implications. Keegan got up to go. Cy was already on his feet. "Mr. Grice, if you hire investigators, let us know who they are."

Grice said nothing. He did not come to the door to see them out of his office.

In the lobby, Madeleva was less radiant, as if she could tell they had not brought good news. Joe Walsh limped ahead to the outside door and pulled it open for them.

"How did it go, Keegan?"

"He refused to let you come back," Keegan said, then punched Walsh in the arm. Walsh did the same to Cy, so they were even as they went out to the car. Keegan waited until Cy was clear of the parking lot and picking up traction on the snowy street before he said anything.

"What do you think, Cy?"

Cy did not like to speculate on inadequate data. But he had been trained to be cautious, trained by Keegan himself. Cy's Hungarian stolidity alone would have been enough to keep him from popping off theories. Keegan had the sinking feeling that it would be extremely difficult to pin anything on Grice.

"What have we got, Cy? A woman missing nearly three months now. Apparently the Grices got along, but half of the company is hers and it could be his alone. And there is the young woman, Pamela Mather."

Cy added, "Who stands to gain a lot, too."

"What do you mean?"

"What I said."

Maybe the *Trib* reporter only had it half right. His insinuation had been that Grice and the young lady had done away with Mrs. Grice. Well, the young lady had motive enough on her own. Cy might not say that aloud and neither would Keegan, but it was worth thinking about.

Phil Keegan was surprised Agnes Lamb hadn't thought of it.

Ten

ggie Miller's funeral was an event. The snow stopped falling and the sun came out but the temperature stood at twenty degrees Fahrenheit, a clear, crisp, midwestern winter day. From the pulpit, Father Dowling looked out at the elderly people filling pew after pew, Aggie's companions from the St. Hilary parish center. He had the feeling these mourners would be here even if a blizzard still raged outside.

In the front pew, directly below the pulpit, sat Barbara Shire, Aggie's daughter. Beside her was her husband, Gerald, a small, precise man whose thin hair was distributed over his head as if by a whirlwind. Two Shire children, a boy and a girl, sat uncomfortably beside their parents. While he had the immediate family in mind as he spoke, Roger Dowling was of the old school as far as homilies at funerals were concerned. No eulogies, no direct address to the bereaved. Better to speak to everyone. After all, all men are mortal.

At the wake the previous night there had been a similar crowd. "Mom always complained that she had no friends and nothing to do," Barbara said, puzzled, looking at the jammed rows in the viewing room.

"Everyone liked her."

"Are they all from the parish? I don't recognize anyone."

"Most of them are regulars at the parish center."

"Mom did like going there."

"She also liked visiting with you and your family in Elgin."

Barbara closed both eyes. "Imagine thinking of a few days in Elgin as a treat."

"I think she enjoyed the shopping."

Barbara looked toward the front of the room, where her mother lay in a coffin flanked by flowers. "We had a lot of fun." She faced Father Dowling. "It's so awful. A long life and then to have it end like that."

There wasn't much to say to that. Gerald made a thin line of his lips and put his arm around his wife. He was a head shorter than Barbara and looked closer to tears than she did, but it was a tender gesture.

It was after the rosary had been said and Aggie's friends had made a last visit to the coffin, briefly holding Barbara's hand and then going off to their long thoughts, that the topic of the ring had come up.

"I want it," Barbara said.

"Have you talked to the police about it?"

"Even if it did belong to someone else, Mother bought it and I think it should be mine."

Roger Dowling recalled Aggie telling him that her daughter had wanted the ring at least as much as she had. It would take a Solomon to figure out who had a right to the ring. Unless Arthur Grice maintained that the ring had been stolen, Barbara could claim she had bought it. Thus far the police had had no luck discovering who, precisely, had sold the ring.

The sale last October had been a neighborhood one, with anyone able to put out a sign or set up a table in the blocked-off street. There was reason to believe that more than one vendor had simply set up without clearing it with the organizers and paying a fee.

"It wasn't exactly a charity thing," Phil Keegan said. "But all the participants put in twenty dollars, and that was to go to Little League basketball."

"Basketball?"

"It's something new, Roger. The neighborhood is young families, lots of kids. I don't think the sale was the most organized in the world. But they did advertise it in the local paper and it was a huge success."

The suggestion seemed to be that someone from outside the neighborhood could have set up a booth and sold things, including the ring, and there was no way to trace it.

"I suppose the police will keep the ring for the time being."

"Do they really think someone killed my mother over that ring?"

"It's at least a possibility."

"But who? The husband?" She meant Arthur Grice. "Why don't they arrest him?"

The Miller house had been dusted for fingerprints, without much hope—there had been none on the handle of the butcher knife. From the tracks through the snow, casts had been made. Arthur Grice had been indignant at the suggestion that any footwear of his would match those tracks, but he had permitted the police to check.

"Which means either he's innocent or he had the sense to get rid of them," said Keegan.

In a side pew of the church sat Cy Horvath, who was here on duty. This seemed a time when not even the wildest chance could be ruled out, and Cy expected that the man who had murdered Aggie Miller, out of morbidity or guilt or maybe the desire to be apprehended, would also be here. What on earth would Cy look for?

Whatever or whoever it was, he was still looking when the funeral reached its grim destination at the cemetery. In this cold, actual burial would have to be postponed, so the final obsequies for Aggie were held in a cemetery chapel, which gave the funeral an unfinished character.

When he said good-bye to the Shires, Father Dowling asked if they were going immediately back to Elgin. Gerald answered. Barbara, who had obviously been trying to withhold her feelings—trying too hard, Father Dowling thought—had now given herself up to healing grief. In her wide, tear-filled eyes was the recognition that she would never see her mother again, that Aggie was no longer there, at the other end of a telephone wire or a short drive from Elgin. The death of a parent, particularly of one's last parent, is never an easy thing.

From the front seat of McDivitt's hearse, Roger Dowling watched the little family go to their car, Barbara leaning on her husband, her cheek crushing his hat. The children followed their parents, awkward and awed by the death of their grandmother.

"When it rains, it pours," Marie Murkin said when he got back to the house.

"That's snow, Marie."

She ignored that. "Mrs. Loring called. It's her father."

"Has something happened?"

"He's had a serious relapse."

Marie handed him the mug she had been holding.

"What's this?"

"Cocoa. You're going to have to go back out into that cold."

He sipped the cocoa. There was no polite way he could refuse this intended kindness. Cocoa was a campaign with Marie, an attempt to wean him from coffee. She was a poet when describing its nutritive and restorative qualities. After wavering under the onslaught of repeated mugs of hot cocoa with tiny marshmallows afloat, Roger Dowling's original distaste for the beverage had returned. Going again into the cold was not as unwelcome as it might have been.

Paul Loring arrived at the nursing home at the same time as Father Dowling, and they walked together from the parking lot.

"Sounds bad, Father."

"When did it happen?"

"I just got the message." He tapped a beeper on his belt, visible under his open fur-lined car coat. He wore a flannel shirt, open at the neck, and clay mixed with the snow on his boots. "I'm putting up a house on King Lake."

"In this weather?"

Paul Loring laughed. "Construction isn't tied to weather the way it used to be."

"I remember my father dreading winter."

"Was he a builder?"

"A plumbing and heating contractor."

Loring skipped up the steps to open the door. Roger Dowling wished he had mentioned his father earlier. It seemed to remove a barrier.

Willis Wirth was on both oxygen and IV and seemed to have shrunk since the last time Roger Dowling had seen him. The skin was tighter on his skull, and his eyes were large when he opened them at the sound of his daughter's voice greeting Father Dowling. Audrey Loring stood and stepped back from the bed, and the priest took the old man's hand. The dry lips moved, and Roger Dowling leaned over.

"The hour of my death," Willis whispered.

It had been a month since Willis had been given the last rites, and Roger Dowling proceeded to anoint the old man again, saying the prayers of the occasion. The Lorings stood together at the foot of the bed, following the ceremony solemnly, but Willis watched everything as if determined to engrave it in his mind and remember it accurately later.

· 63 ·

From Aggie Miller's funeral to assisting Willis Wirth in his final minutes on earth—not every day had such finality, not even for the pastor of St. Hilary's, the average age of whose parishioners was over fifty. It seemed Willis had followed as closely as he had in order to be in on the end of his own life. Roger Dowling was reading the final prayer when the old man breathed his last.

Audrey did not at first understand what had happened. For months her father had been in the process of dying. It took half a minute before she realized it was all over.

"What I feel is relief that he won't have to suffer anymore."

"He's at rest now," the priest said.

"Will you say the funeral Mass?"

"Of course."

Paul Loring was staring at his father-in-law, his face expressionless except for a pained look in his eyes. He seemed to come to.

"Is it still McDivitt's, Father Dowling?"

He meant the funeral home. "Not necessarily. Would you prefer someone else?"

"No. McDivitt is fine." He looked at his wife and she nodded.

"I've just come from there."

"Another funeral?"

"Aggie Miller."

Audrey's mouth opened and closed. "The woman who was murdered?"

"It drew a great crowd."

"Have they found who did it?"

"I don't believe so."

Paul Loring said, "Willis outlived all his friends, Father. There won't be many at his funeral."

Eleven

And then the games began. That is how Captain Phillip Keegan thought of them, as goddamn games, but he was not even remotely amused.

The disappearance of Frances Grice was one of those things that was more nothing than something, an absence that might or might not be significant. The media had swung from being sympathetic to Arthur Grice to all but accusing him of getting rid of his wife in order to be free for Pamela Mathers, the administrative director of Grice Enterprises. Keegan had never been able to make up his mind about Arthur Grice.

On the one hand, there was reason to think that his marriage had been what he, and until recently almost everyone else, said it was: happy, solid, successful. Given that, his abject reaction had to be considered sincere, as well as his anger at the fact that it had taken so long for anything to turn up.

The ring put things in a different light. There was no doubt that it belonged to the missing woman. Her husband said she had been wearing it on September 25, and there seemed to be no basis for doubting that Aggie Miller and her daughter, Mrs. Shire, had bought it at a garage sale in Elgin in mid-October. And, even though the ring had been found on the body of Aggie Miller, it seemed plausible that the ring had been the object of the break-in. That Aggie was dead and the ring unstolen made the episode seem doubly insane.

It was Cy Horvath who pointed out what should have been obvious. There seemed to be more than one person involved. It made no sense to think that the person who had sold the ring in Elgin was the same one who had killed Aggie Miller and ransacked her bedroom in a futile effort to find it.

So now they had two unknown persons involved in the disappearance of a woman.

"Two might be enough, Captain."

"How so?"

"One could be the woman."

Frances Grice? That possibility was destroyed by a phone call. Anonymous. Reporting the discovery of a woman's body.

The call came in at one in the morning, and the sergeant who took the message had sense enough to phone the chief of detectives. Phil Keegan was a fitful sleeper at best, but with this kind of problem his sleep was shallow. Not so shallow, though, that he didn't think he was dreaming.

"Where?"

"Out on Route 19."

"Where the hell on Route 19? That road is fifty miles long."

It was near Barrington. The caller had seen the body in the back of a pickup truck.

Keegan called Cy before leaving his apartment. He went unshaven and untied to the location, breathing deeply to get oxygen to his brain, and listening to the radio full blast. The sleep that had been eluding him all night tugged at his eyelids now and filled him with lassitude. Twice he nodded off for only an instant and snapped to as the car drifted toward the side of the road. The second time, his pulling on the wheel nearly sent the car into a spin.

The body of a woman. He realized he did not have a doubt in the world that this meant Frances Grice. He followed the road right into Barrington without finding anything and continued on through, kicking himself for not asking which side of Barrington. A few miles out of town. Going away from Barrington was hard, because he had the crazy thought that he had missed it and was putting more and more miles between himself and what he was looking for.

And then he saw the lights ahead, the rotators, the unmistakable signs of officers of the law. There were two state police cruisers, a deputy sheriff and a constable from the town of Barrington. The Fox River cruiser was the first in line, meaning the last to arrive. Keegan stayed in the road and rolled to a stop beside a cluster of cops holding a caucus on the berm. He held up his ID.

"Where's the truck?"

He knew from the way each of them waited for someone else to answer that something was wrong. He got out of the car and nearly fell. He was wearing his bedroom slippers and on the ice could not get traction. Williams crunched over the crusty snow to him and took his arm, and thus assisted Keegan joined the group.

"It was here," the deputy said.

"What do you mean was?"

Williams lifted his arm and Keegan shook free, but had to grab hold again when his feet started to go out from under him. "Tell me what the hell is going on!" he demanded.

They all spoke at once. The fact that there were tracks showing that a truck had actually been there was emphasized, as if this justified half a dozen grown men standing around on a county road in the middle of the night. They stood there, making sure Keegan didn't know everything they didn't know, shining lights on the tire treads etched in the crusty snow at the road's edge. It was Williams who'd found the shoe.

A woman's shoe. Blue leather, medium-height heel, fairly new, although there were signs of wear. The make and size were legible. Would the shoe belong to Frances Grice? No one speculated about who the caller was or whose shoe this was. No one actually said that the shoe Williams had found and the alleged body in the alleged truck were connected, but Keegan bet everyone else had made at least that jump. So maybe they were thinking of Mrs. Grice, too.

He was thinking of Cinderella, remembering reading the story to his daughters when they were little girls, pained that such vivid memories were of events so long past, but even more pained by the thought that some son of a bitch was playing games with law-enforcement units from four different jurisdictions. Who would get the shoe became a matter of discussion.

Keegan won the half-hour-long argument punctuated by people calling in for instructions. It was like an international conference, with diplomats unable to speak on their own authority. That gave Keegan the advantage.

"It's evidence in a crime we are investigating."

"How do you know that?"

"Look at the label."

The shoe was passed around and the label studied. Keegan said, "That shoe was worn by Frances Grice when she disappeared in late September. We are investigating her disappearance as a possible homicide. This shoe is crucial."

Nothing on the label justified the claim that the shoe belonged to Frances Grice. Perhaps the others wanted an honorable way to get into their vehicles and get out of there.

"You say last September?" the Barrington constable asked. His uniform was the gaudiest one there. "This shoe hasn't been outside that long."

"You bet it hasn't. That's my point."

The constable took this as praise and let it go. Williams and the constable helped Keegan back to his car. He closed the door and rolled down the window, indicating he wanted the two men to stick around. The sheriff's cruisers went off in opposite directions, and the state cop drove half a mile down the road before turning on his lights. Suddenly it was very quiet. And Keegan's feet were very cold.

"Williams, I want you to stay right here. Cy Horvath will be along very soon. I want you to see if those tire tracks lead anywhere. Cy will have an impression taken first. Constable, would you certify that sample?"

The man nodded. On the front of his ten-gallon hat a giant official shield was mounted. Keegan had difficulty reading the number: 0003. He bet there weren't many more than three people entitled to wear that uniform.

Phil didn't wait for Cy to get there, but reached him on the radio and told him what he would find when he went a few miles past Barrington on Route 19. "Williams," Cy said, and that was all.

Williams was on this shift just because of what Cy's tone suggested.

"I've got the shoe with me. As soon as possible in the morning, I will be calling on Grice."

"You want me to call before then if something comes up?"

"The reason I'm leaving, Cy, besides there not being anything there, is my feet are freezing. I was in such a hurry to get going I went out in my slippers."

Back in his apartment, Phil lay the blue shoe on its side on the top of his television set and went back to bed. He fell asleep as if he were dropping down an elevator shaft.

Twelve

Williams sat yawning in the car by the side of the road, sipping a can of warm coke. He looked at Cy for several beats before lurching upright behind the wheel, as if what he had thought was a mirage now proved itself to be a flesh and blood lieutenant. He managed to get the door open, rolled out of the car, and got his feet positioned.

"Keegan was wearing slippers," he said, watching Cy to see if he would think it a joke.

"Where are the tracks?"

Cy followed the beam of Williams's flashlight and stood over the deeply embedded imprint of the tire tread, and then traced them back to where they turned off the road and onto the shoulder. Except for the tracks, which had been made by one front and one rear wheel, the side of the road was an unmarked expanse of snow with a thin crust of glaze.

"Where was the shoe?"

"Just lying there." Williams pointed.

Cy supposed that an object as light as a shoe could lie on

top of the snow without making a mark. He had left his head-lights on and their beams illumed the scene. What the hell did it mean? He got in beside Williams and heard the story. A telephone call pinpointing the location of the truck, reporting the body of a woman in the bed of the truck.

"Anyone in the cab?"

"Didn't say. Keegan said the body was that missing woman. Mrs. Grice."

Cy wondered if Keegan had any reason other than hope that finally they were getting a break on the disappearance. And so it seemed. Agnes Lamb was given what she called the Cinderella Detail, and by early afternoon had established that the shoe had been bought by Frances Grice in a boutique in a Lake Forest mall. There were dozens of stores in the western sub-urbs that carried the line of shoes, and Agnes did as she was trained to do, started at the top and worked to the bottom. Once the purchase had been established, Keegan and Agnes paid a call on Arthur Grice. This is why Cy Horvath was alone when the call came in. The second call.

"The boat house," the muffled male voice said when the call was switched to Cy.

"No, this is police headquarters."

A pause. "The woman's body? It's in the Grice boat house."

The line went dead. Cy put down the phone and stared at it. Keegan had referred to the earlier call as a game. Agnes ob-viously thought taking a shoe around to women's boutiques was a kind of fairy tale. Now this.

In school you would come upon a scribbled note. "Turn to p. 66." On page sixty-six was a note telling you to turn to page thirteen. And so you skipped back and forth through the book until you came to the payoff. Sucker! Cy wondered if everyone turned the pages as he had. There was always the possibility that this time it was different. And there was only one way to find out.

That was how it was going to be with this, and it might all end in that taunting cry. Sucker! But they had to find out.

The Grice estate, seen from the river, seemed designed to take advantage of its commanding site on the west bank of the Fox River. Seen from the road, it seemed equally to have been constructed in terms of the road. Cy had seen it from both vantage points. One Sunday afternoon he and his wife boarded a sight-seeing craft that featured an elaborate if nonfunctional paddle wheel. On weekends the boat took passengers up and down the river—picnickers, lovers, those just enjoying the hypnotic effect of being on water, particularly with a six-pack of beer. The slow-motion passage by the Grice place was more suggestive of the South than of Illinois.

"Is that a slave cabin?" Lilian asked, pointing to the boat house. It was reached by a snow white stairway that came in flights down the bluff, punctuated by platforms with lamps and benches. The squat boat house extended into the river and opened onto it. A launch and a powerboat moved in the wake of the passing tour boat. Moored to a buoy to the right of the boat house was a double-hulled cat whose bobbing mast seemed to be trying to sight in on the house above. What did a boat house look like in winter?

Now there was ice on the river, especially on the west bank, and even the unfrozen water looked gelid. Cy stood on a marina on the east bank, his binoculars moving systematically over the boat house.

The stairway looked as if it had not been swept clean of snow since the beginning of winter, and he could see no sign that anyone had come down them. Nor was there any indication around the boat house itself that anyone had been in or around it—to deposit a body brought by truck, for instance. Cy felt as if he had just turned to the third page and was being instructed to continue a silly search.

"Can you take me across, Foley?"

Foley looked after the marina during the winter in exchange

for lodging. He and a very fat dog had been snoozing about four feet from a space heater that looked like a fire hazard to Cy. A kerosene burner, its flame radiated by a reflector, heated the room and toasted anything within a six-foot range of that reflector. But Foley had on a coat sweater over his turtleneck, and a scarf twisted around his throat. He looked as if he had just been let down from the gallows. He studied Cy with one eye before deciding to open the other.

"We're closed." He had opened the second eye when Cy showed his ID. Awake, he looked at the TV murmuring in a corner out of range of the heater. One of the soaps that Lilian watched despite herself. The dog's tail began to thump on the floor when he saw that this intruder had not alarmed Foley.

"I want to use your dock."

"You took a boat out today?" The old man seemed to think he had arrived by sea, not by land.

"That may be a good idea."

One corner of Foley's mouth lifted and he studied Cy for clues.

"Can you see the Grice place from the dock?"

"You can see it from the back window. There's coffee on."

"No thanks." A yellowing electric percolator with a cloudy pot sent out fumes more pungent than the heater's. The red light indicating the machine was on seemed a warning against drinking the coffee.

"How do I get out on the dock?"

"Is this official or something?"

"I'm not on vacation, Foley."

Foley came with him as far as the door, but he and the dog stayed inside.

Having studied the Grice boat house enough to know he could determine nothing more about the dock than he already had, Cy turned and went back inside.

"I could see it from in here," Foley said.

"I'm going to want a boat. But first I have to make a phone call."

"A boat!"

"This is a marina, isn't it?"

"Sure it is. It's also December and damned near Christmas. You wanna go swimming, too?"

"You think we'll need divers?"

"Lieutenant, I don't know what the hell you're talking about."

Cy wasn't all that sure himself, but he knew he wanted at least Keegan in on this, and maybe some others. When they turned the last page and saw Sucker, he didn't want to be alone.

He was told Keegan had not yet returned, so he called Grice's office. The receptionist's voice even sounded Ethiopian.

"Mr. Grice is not in."

"This is Lieutenant Horvath."

"You already said that."

"Has Captain Keegan been there?"

"Yes."

"When was that?"

She seemed to give the whole conversation some thought and then said, "He left with Mr. Grice."

"Where did they go?"

"I believe Mr. Grice was going home."

Cy ducked down and squinted across the river. Was Keegan in the house? He got the number and after several frosty minutes with underlings who did not sound like Ethiopians, Keegan came on the line.

"We've had another call."

"Yeah?"

"I am at the marina directly across from the Grice boat house. The caller said we would find the missing body there."

"You're across the river?"

"I am going to cross by boat. There are stairs that lead down from the house. I'll meet you there. You might want to call the ME."

"Do you believe the caller?"

"We found a shoe this morning."

"It's hers, Cy."

"Maybe the body is, too."

Once the dog got outside, he liked it. How long had it been since he had breathed fresh air? He loped around in the snow, lay down and rolled around in it, then waddled toward Foley, his whole rear end happy. Foley had pulled on a sheepskin and a leather hat that came down low over his head, had flaps, and tied with a string beneath the chin of your choice.

"Look at the water," Foley whined.

"A rowboat will do."

"I wouldn't put an outboard in that ice water for anything."

"I'll row."

"What you need me for?"

"Protection."

"Come on."

"A witness. Who knows what we'll find in the Grice boat house?"

"Boats."

"Have you seen anyone over there, Foley? I mean in the last couple months."

"My job is to watch the marina, not the goddamn Grice boat house." Foley embraced himself as if he were his own last friend. It was maybe fifteen degrees out and there wasn't much of a breeze, but Foley looked as if he were standing on a glacier in Little America.

When he rowed away from the marina dock, he had the choice of looking at Foley's sullen face, gloved hands gripping the sides of the boat, or at the dog standing quizzically on the dock, tipping his head now to one side, now to the other. Cy chose the dog. And from time to time, he looked over his shoulder toward his destination. He brought the boat sideways when he saw the figures starting down the stairway. He wished he had made Foley row. But he was certain one of the figures was Keegan. The woman would be Agnes Lamb. The large figure leading them down looked like Arthur Grice.

The progress of the boat was slow because of a very active current that took everything Cy had to work against it, but even so he should have beat the three coming down the stairs. The problem was the ice, which was just thick enough to be a nuisance, and he had to ram into it with the prow of the boat—back off, ram it again. It got thicker the closer to shore he got. Twenty yards from the boat house, he could hear Keegan talking as he came down the steps, but they still had a long way to go on the large zigzag of a stairway.

"The boat house is locked," Foley said, sounding undecided whether to cry or laugh.

"Well, it's closed."

"It's locked."

"That's the owner coming down from the house."

Foley was so absorbed in his own misery that he had not noticed the three coming down the stairs.

"Is that who you called?"

Keegan was speaking to him now, and Cy shipped the oars and looked up. Were they making such slow progress because Grice was setting the pace?

Six feet from shore, Cy stepped onto the ice and held the side of the boat. "Get out, Foley, and we'll pull it out of the water."

"I'm not getting on that ice." Foley looked terrified, and it occurred to Cy that Foley had a lot more experience of the winter river than he did. He moved rapidly across the ice to the shore, or where the shore must have been under a foot of snow. He decided he really didn't need Foley.

"Take the boat back, Foley. I can get a ride around to my car."

This alternative frightened Foley almost as much as the ice.

On the far dock, the dog began to howl. Cy went back out on the ice and pushed the boat. It went out into the channel he had made through the thinner ice. Foley's grip on the sides of the boat tightened.

"You son of a bitch."

Cy couldn't really blame Foley. He hadn't been much companionship on the crossing, and with Keegan and Agnes on the scene there was no need for Foley. The watchman began very gingerly to change seats.

Cy waited until Foley was in the center seat, had his gloves on the oars, and was rowing back toward his dog and the warmth of his heater. Cy then began to trudge through the snow to where the others would arrive.

"I closed this boat house in September," Grice said angrily when he reached the bottom. He was wearing street shoes, and the bottoms of his trousers were white with snow. "It's pretty goddamn obvious nobody has been down here."

Keegan put out a hand to help Agnes down the final steps. He spoke over his shoulder to Grice.

"The boat house locked?"

"Of course it's locked!"

"You remember to bring the key?"

Cy had the impression that the two men had been wrangling throughout the long descent. Agnes rolled her eyes. Grice came up to Cy and stood toe to toe. "What the hell is supposed to be in the boat house."

"A body."

Grice was mad, no doubt about that, and who could blame him? On the other hand, it was his wife who was missing and the possibility that there was a body of a woman in the boat house should mean more to him than to anyone. Maybe that was why he was so mad.

"Doesn't look like anyone's been around here," Keegan admitted. "What's the water side look like, Cy?"

"Undisturbed."

"Undisturbed," Grice repeated as if some record for idiotic remarks had just been set.

He got the key into the lock, pulled the door toward him, and turned the key. Then he pushed the door into darkness. Grice reached in, flicked a switch and waited for Keegan to go first. Phil lowered a shoulder as if the door were still closed and locked, and disappeared inside. Sucker? It couldn't have been half a minute before Keegan looked out at them.

"Bingo," he said.

Inside the boat house, two large craft had been lifted free and hung from the ceiling, suspended by large canvas straps. A kind of balcony ran around the inside of the boat house. Keegan led them around the boats to the far side of the building, and pointed downward.

The lights Grice had snapped on illuminated the ice below, which was smooth as a mirror, very clear. It took a moment to realize it wasn't a reflection.

The canoe had been sunk in maybe three feet of water and was very visible through the ice. So was the nude body of the woman lying in it, her limbs disposed modestly, her hands crossed over her breast.

Cy looked at Grice, who stared openmouthed at the frozen canoe and its occupant. His lips formed a word.

Frankie.

Thirteen

She would have preferred to remember the weddings, the first communions, even the confirmations when they had a bishop in the house, but what always stuck in Marie Murkin's mind were the funerals.

It was an occupational hazard, she supposed. How could you take care of a rectory and avoid the sad things in life? But funerals weren't just sad things; they were the saddest. People with troubles, no matter how down they were when they came to Father Dowling, came because they thought there was hope.

"The main thing standing between people and happiness is usually their will."

She remembered that, maybe because she hadn't quite understood it when Father Dowling had said it. Now she did. Who isn't his own worst enemy? No one can make us do the dumb things we do. We're free not to do them. So who do we have to blame if we act stupidly? It made a lot of sense. Even so, Father Dowling didn't appreciate it if she tried to save him some time, and she told people so.

"You cook and I'll be pastor," he had told her more than once. As if he could cook.

Willis Wirth's funeral was more than sad, it was pathetic. McDivitt tried to talk them into a public viewing at the funeral home, but Father Dowling vetoed that. Instead, the coffin was opened in the back of the church for half an hour before the Mass. Edna Hospers came, representing the parish center, but Willis hadn't been there all that often. Even so, if a new blizzard hadn't blown into Fox River, some of the old folks would have been there, but every radio and TV station was telling people to stay put, to avoid unnecessary driving. Schools and businesses closed.

"I opened," Edna whispered to Marie. "Forbes is minding things."

"He ought to be shoveling snow."

"Marie, he isn't an employee. He volunteers."

"I didn't mean it that way." Marie glanced sideways at the sharp features of Willis Wirth emerging from the silk-lined casket.

"He is clearing the walks, though. All I told him was to be on the lookout and let people know the doors are unlocked."

They closed the casket. McDivitt and a sallow assistant who reeked of cigarette smoke pushed it up the aisle, a little fast, Marie thought, and the Lorings followed. Marie and Edna came next. Father Dowling, vested for Mass, awaited them on the sanctuary step.

Marie felt that they were all engaged in an illicit act. Strange how certain things, the important things, had to be public. When a couple fell in love, which was nobody's business but theirs, Marie felt, they needed a license, they got married, everybody had to be told. Because of the kids, because of the obligations that came with kids, that seemed to be the reason. Death seemed about as private a thing as there was, but one needed a certificate and then a ceremony. Why? The wonder that attended it, certainly, but Marie bet a lot of it had to do with making sure a person had died of natural causes, and hadn't been killed.

The Lorings had waited a long time for Audrey's father to lay down his burden, or to remove theirs, or both (to be fair), but Marie could not imagine anyone killing Willis Wirth.

The first time he visited the rectory, he stared at the crucifixes in each room and at the statue of the Curé d'Ars Father Dowling had in the visiting room, where Willis was to wait for the pastor.

"Do you adore those things?" the old man asked.

"Don't be silly."

"I'm just asking a question."

Apparently he was. He was fascinated by everything Catholic but had the oddest notions. He had been certain Catholics believed in rebirth.

"You mean baptism?"

"I mean coming back to another life here on earth."

"One's enough."

His laugh was a kind of cackle. "You're right. 'A time to live and a time to die.' Who said that?"

"Don't be silly."

"I'm just asking a question."

Asking questions about religion was the way Willis Wirth spent his last year and a half on earth. Maybe people would scoff at someone getting religion when he has cancer but who isn't dying?

They were on their way out of the church so quickly Marie realized her mind had been wandering all over the place during the service. Well, she had been thinking of Willis, sort of, and besides, just being there meant something.

Outside the church, McDivitt and the assistant, who seemed to have been out in the weather smoking during the service, carried the casket to the hearse. Father Dowling joined them, and the Lorings pulled their car up behind the hearse.

"What a way to go," Marie said to Edna, who nodded in agreement.

The cars pulled away. It was then that Marie became conscious of the motor. Forbes came into view, a great spume of snow from the blower arching into the street.

"He loves that machine," Edna said.

"It's a toy."

"Thank God he likes to play. And he said he didn't want Father to buy one."

"Come have some cocoa."

"Do you have coffee?"

"Do you know what's in a cup of coffee, Edna?"

"Cream and sugar, I hope."

Marie put on the coffee, if only for the company. Besides, she wanted a cup herself and now that Father Dowling was out she wouldn't be a bad example by drinking one.

She winced when Edna loaded up her cup with sugar and cream. Didn't the woman read *Reader's Digest*?

"How long is this snow supposed to go on?"

Marie turned on the radio to WBBM. That is when they heard it. It didn't seem right that they should have received the news that way.

The body of Mrs. Frances Grice, the Fox River woman who had been missing for several months, had been found in the boat house of the family estate. Frozen. In a sunken boat. Without any clothes on. Marie's mouth opened wider at each outrage.

The phone rang. It was Captain Keegan asking for Father Dowling.

"They just found the body," she said.

"Roger's?"

"Honestly! Mrs. Grice's. It was on the news."

"I was there when it was found, Marie. Where's Roger?"

"Burying the dead. Willis Wirth's funeral was this morning."

"I'm sorry to hear that. When do you expect him back?"

"At the general resurrection."

"You need a vacation, Marie."

"Tell me about finding Mrs. Grice's body."

"I'll come to lunch and tell you then."

He just hung up. Marie nodded a time or two, said good-bye to the dead phone and hung it up.

"That was Captain Keegan. He found the body."

Edna said nothing. Then Marie remembered that Edna did not care for Phil Keegan. Or for Cy Horvath, either. Well, who could blame her? It was easier to be mad at the police than at her husband, who was in prison in Joliet.

"He's coming over."

That hastened Edna's departure, as Marie expected. What she hoped was that Captain Keegan would come before Father Dowling returned and tell her all about it before she had to be busy with lunch and miss every other sentence.

The prospect of hearing of the discovery of Mrs. Grice's body brightened her day, despite the swirling snow at the window. She needed a lift.

Fourteen

Mrs. Loring had a lost look when it was all over, and it was a pity there were no relatives or friends there to make it easier for her. There is such finality in leaving the grave of a parent, no matter how elderly. Roger Dowling imagined that for the first time she really felt her age. He had been affected thus by his mother's death. There was no longer the buffer of an older generation between himself and the grave.

"Can we give you a lift back to the rectory?" Paul Loring asked.

"Thanks," he said, waving to McDivitt and his assistant, indicating he would not be going with them.

Audrey Loring insisted on sitting in back, so Roger Dowling got in next to her husband.

"Dad left you some money, Father."

"Oh?"

"He was really very grateful to you. So am I."

Paul Loring cleared his throat and nodded, as if to include himself in the remark.

"It's quite a lot of money," Audrey said.

The subject of money always made Roger Dowling uneasy, and he was particularly uneasy to think that Willis might have bequeathed him money that should have gone to his family. Had that been the reason for offering to drive him back to the rectory?

"He should have left his money to you."

"Oh, he did. Most of it."

Paul Loring said, "The sum he gave to St. Hilary's is fifty thousand dollars."

"Good heavens. I had no idea he had so much money."

Audrey laughed. "Dad was quite well off, Father Dowling."

He must have been, if he could leave the parish fifty thousand dollars and leave still more to the Lorings.

"Of course, it has to go through probate," Paul said. "Leave it to the lawyers to delay matters."

"Well, this is a surprise."

"You gave him an awful lot of time, Father," Audrey said. "You earned it."

"Of course, there are things the parish could do with such money that it cannot do now."

They approached a slippery intersection. The light changed against them, and when Loring applied the brakes there was no immediate result. They slid eerily toward the intersection, where cars were now moving to the right and left across their path. A dry spot saved them, giving the wheels traction, and they came to a stop only a few feet past where they normally would have. Paul Loring was gripping the wheel, chin thrust forward, shoulders rounded, a picture of tension.

"God is my copilot," he murmured.

Roger laughed. "You can't be old enough to remember that."

"He's a World War II buff," Audrey said. "Don't get him started."

"It's my hobby, Father. Some like the Civil War. Mine is World War II."

It got them off the subject of money, at least until they got to the rectory. "Amos Cadbury will get in touch with you, Father," Audrey said, and when the priest went blank, added, "He was Dad's lawyer. He'll put the will through probate."

Roger Dowling nodded, got out of the car, and opened the back door so Audrey could move up front with her husband. He took her gloved hand to say good-bye, as a precaution— nowadays women had the disturbing habit of wanting to kiss priests. Then he went inside and heard about Frances Grice.

"Captain Keegan is coming for lunch."

"Does he know I won't be saying a noon Mass?"

There was a hollow noise as Marie clapped a hand over her open mouth. "I forgot to tell him."

"I'll try to reach him. Otherwise we can just have lunch at the usual time."

As it turned out he would have no lunch at all. Since Roger Dowling was free, Phil suggested they run out to the Grice boat house before the scene was disturbed.

Looking down at the ice-enclosed canoe and the body in it, Roger was reminded vaguely of ancient burial customs. The pyramids? He wasn't sure, perhaps because he was more powerfully reminded of contemporary associations whose members wanted to be frozen for possible future resuscitation. Why was the future so attractive? Today was tomorrow only yesterday. But this frozen body made one eager to know the past, not the future. What would Frances Grice tell them if thawing could revive her?

"Don't say she looks like she's sleeping," Phil said beside him.

"Why not?"

"That's what everyone says."

"They're probably right."

"Yeah."

"Of course you will have to be careful raising the body temperature. Electric shock will help."

"Then we can put a bolt through her neck."

"She does look peaceful. I don't see signs of violence, do you?"

"Other than being drowned in a freezing river?"

"Touché. Is that the matching shoe?"

"It looks like it."

The cadaver's legs were crossed and the top foot was clad in a blue shoe whose heel was not overly high.

The scene had been photographed and captured on video film. Keegan gave the okay and two officers in frogmen outfits were lowered to the ice and began to chip away, starting the delicate task of freeing the boat and its cargo. Roger and Phil Keegan watched for a time, but the operation was now under the command of Kite and the ME staff, making Keegan feel like a kibitzer.

When they were on the way back to Phil's car, the message came.

Phil snatched up the radio and called in. Roger jumped into the car beside him. The message was confirmed. Arthur Grice had attempted suicide at his office.

"That's where I'll be," Phil said, and switched out. He refused to use the conventional on and off words of radio communication.

They drove in silence and at an unsafe rate of speed, given the slippery, snow-packed streets. Roger Dowling tried not to think of all the news stories of emergency vehicles involved in fatal traffic accidents. The thought of being killed in an ambulance while being taken to emergency had an irony he might have appreciated in his study, but not sitting next to Phil in the careening car, its siren going full blast.

It was Madeleva, Grice's secretary, who had discovered him in time to save his life. Unable to get through to him about incoming calls, she had overcome her reluctance to just open the door of the inner office and look in. Thus she had found Arthur Grice slumped over his desk. She had immediately dialed the emergency number. The bottle of aspirin lying empty on the desk beside the Styrofoam cup half full of Coke prompted the stomach pump that kept Arthur Grice on this side of the grim boundary between the quick and the dead.

Madeleva was at the hospital and so was Pamela Mathers, giving Father Dowling the opportunity to meet two women Phil had spoken of. Pamela, of course, was someone of whom he had read as well.

"Is aspirin fatal?" Roger Dowling asked the Indian intern.

He thought a moment. "Almost anything taken in sufficient amounts is."

"How much had he taken?"

"We will have to await the analysis."

Madeleva stood with serene composure in the room where the resident explained this to Keegan. Pamela Mathers looked shaken by the events of the past several hours, and Roger Dowling suggested they go for coffee. She looked up at him, an outdoor girl with her nicely weathered skin, clear eyes, and helmet of hair. She nodded and came along with him.

"He hadn't wanted to believe that Frankie was dead. As long as her body wasn't found, he could think she was alive."

"Of course her death would be a shock, even with months of thinking of it as a possibility."

"He never admitted it was possible."

"What explanation did he have?"

She looked at him. "None. He really didn't understand."

"You knew the wife?"

"Yes." She spoke only after seeming to wonder what, if anything, he might have heard of her.

"What do you think happened?"

"Now we know."

"How do you mean?"

"She was kidnapped and murdered."

"Without a demand for ransom?"

They had come to a sitting area where soft drinks and snacks were available in coin-operated machines. Now that they were there she refused a Coke, but sank to a chair and pulled a package of cigarettes from her purse. She looked around.

"I don't see any No Smoking signs."

"I'll join you," he said, taking out a pipe.

"I never told Arthur I smoked. He was such a health nut. I believe in exercise. I know smoking is insane. But I acquired the habit in school. Trying to break it is worse than keeping it."

"Smoking isn't a sin, although it is approaching the status of a crime."

"Here's to crime," she said, inhaling deeply.

"How did you hear about Mrs. Grice? I mean that her body had been found."

"Madeleva called and told me. Arthur had asked her to do that, but she would have anyway."

"There doesn't seem to be any way of telling who might attempt suicide."

"Suicide!"

"Didn't you hear the doctor?"

"I guess it just struck me. But you're right, I would never have thought him the type, even after all this terrible waiting and wondering. He took such meticulous care of his health. The aspirin was part of that."

"Oh?"

"He hadn't taken aspirin for years, he told me, until he read that it prevents heart disease. He's been taking them like vitamins. I mean regularly."

Remembering the intern's remark, Roger wondered if there was such a thing as an overdose of vitamins. Why not? People could kill themselves with food or drink. "Thank God his secretary found him in time."

Pamela nodded, exhaling smoke. "Believe me, Madeleva is essential to Grice Enterprises."

"I've heard the same of you."

"In a different way. Madeleva simplified Arthur's life. Her expression never changes, but she is completely devoted to him. Which is why her salary is what it is."

"High?"

"High. Arthur rewards success."

"He may owe her his life."

Pamela looked away. There seemed a limit to her willingness to praise the willowy Ethiopian. "I wonder when we can talk with him."

"Let's find out."

"You didn't light your pipe."

The room in which they had left Phil Keegan and Madeleva was empty when they returned to it, and there was no sign of the Indian resident. Roger Dowling stopped a nurse.

"Where is Mr. Arthur Grice now?"

"He's been taken to a room in intensive care."

"How do we get there?"

In the elevator Pamela said, "I thought she'd stop us from coming up."

"Priests can go anywhere in hospitals."

"Is that why you came to see Arthur?"

"How do you mean?"

"Don't you give a blessing or something?"

"Was he a practicing Catholic?"

"Can you stop being a Catholic?"

He smiled. "If you don't watch out."

"I'm not Catholic."

He let it go. It was always dangerous to assume people had senses of humor. Keegan was just coming out of Arthur Grice's room. He had left Cy Horvath in there, and now posted a guard. "No visitors," he announced.

Madeleva floated forward. "I must see him for only a moment, Captain Keegan."

Phil shook his head. "No visitors."

"There are important business . . ."

Phil turned away from her. If Madeleva was disappointed or angry there was no way of reading this from her expression. She looked at him for a second or two, turned and glided away from the area. In any case Phil now had Pamela to deal with, but she was no luckier than the secretary had been.

"But how is he?"

"Medically? They tell me he's out of danger."

"Thank God."

"Amen," Phil said, dipping his head toward Roger and beckoning to him as he headed for the elevator.

"Let's get some lunch at Stub's." This was a saloon across from police headquarters. "Or maybe you'd rather not be seen there."

"In the custody of the police?"

"They have the biggest, juiciest, greasiest hamburgers in town, and draft beer, but you can always have soda pop."

Roger Dowling wondered if there was an alternative to the big, juicy, greasy hamburger. There was. It was called a grilled cheese sandwich—partially melted cheese between bread that seemed to have been fried in the same grease as Phil's hamburger.

"He didn't do it," Phil said, speaking with his mouth full.

"It?"

"Try to commit suicide."

"But all that aspirin . . ."

"The damnedest thing, Roger. The analysis turned up no aspirin, although other tests indicated he had taken maybe one."

"So they didn't have to pump his stomach?"

"Wrong. It saved his life. He was full of arsenic."

"Where did he get hold of that?"

"He didn't. My guess is the Coke. Agnes is working on it."

Phil ate with great gusto and far too fast, obviously eager to get back to his office. They parted outside, and Roger went back to the rectory and a pouting Marie Murkin.

"You might have called to tell me."

"Everything happened too fast."

"Everything?"

But they did not have an adequate idea of everything until that night, when Phil showed up claiming a rain check on lunch and wanting dinner.

Fifteen

uke Horowitz could not have found his rear end with both hands. This was Tuttle's considered opinion, and he was not reluctant to tell it to Duke himself or to Peanuts Pianone, the Fox River cop whose presence on the force attested to the political power of the Pianone family. Tuttle thought of Peanuts as enjoying early retirement while still remaining a member of the department. Peanuts had big ears and a closed mouth, but also a weakness for Chinese food. He had been a precious source of information for Tuttle over the years.

Peanuts sat in Tuttle's office eating fried rice from a Styrofoam container, pausing now and then to bring a quart-size container of Pepsi to his mouth.

"Horowitz can't find his rear end with both hands," Tuttle said.

"Has he lost it?"

"He never had it," Tuttle said equivocally.

Peanuts went back to his fried rice. You could never count

on Peanuts to pick up the thread of a conversation, especially while he was eating.

"Grice hired him to follow his poopsy Pamela so I hired *him* to follow Grice."

"Why?"

"What you think happened to Grice's wife?"

"I dunno."

"Look. A guy has a wife and also a young and beautiful girlfriend and the wife disappears, what do you think happened?"

Peanuts looked Tuttle in the eye but said nothing. Did he understand? It was the kind of question that might bother you if you were looking at a chimp in a cage.

"Grice got rid of her," Tuttle said helpfully.

"They found her."

That was how Tuttle learned of the frozen body in the sunken canoe in the Grice boat house. His fried rice went cold as he tried to think what this new development meant. The first thought was that fifty thousand dollars had just gone out the window. On second thought, he wasn't so sure. How had Grice expressed the offer? That was the question, and he would have to check on it. There had to be a way in which Tuttle & Tuttle could lay claim to that reward. So back to the details of the discovery of the body.

"In the river," had been Peanuts's first answer as to where Mrs. Grice had been found. Only later, between gulps of Pepsi, did he specify that the river was inside the Grice boat house.

"Whose canoe?" Peanuts did not understand the question. "The canoe the body was found in, did it belong to Grice?"

Peanuts didn't know. Was this the wedge Tuttle sought? Using the excuse of getting rid of the plastic and paper, he went down the hall with Peanuts and dumped the trash in a plastic bag, and then he went on downstairs. He wanted to use the phone in the lobby. He looked up the Grice number, dialed it, identified himself as a correspondent for the Tuttle

Newsletter, and said, "I'm verifying details on my story about Mrs. Grice. How many canoes does Mr. Grice own?"

"One moment, please."

Tuttle figured this was the old heave-ho but he hung on anyway, and two minutes later another voice came on, with a querulous hello.

"What's the number?"

"The number of what?"

"How many canoes does Mr. Grice own?"

"Canoes? He doesn't own any canoes."

Tuttle replaced the phone as satisfaction surged through him. Thus must Einstein have felt when he worked out that theory about his relatives. A hunch had been pursued and paid off. The canoe had to come from somewhere, and Tuttle was willing to bet that a boat in a boat house would not be the first thing the police looked into. They would assume it belonged there. Tuttle now knew otherwise. And he thought he knew how to pursue the lead.

When he got to the marina he pounded on the door, but despite the fact that a dog inside began to howl and moan, no one came. Where the hell was Foley? Tuttle stepped into the snow and sidled along the wall of the building to a window. He bent and looked inside, and was staring Foley right in the eye.

"Foley! It's me." He pulled the paper sack from his coat pocket and flourished it. "Let me in."

The door was unlocked and opened before he waded back through the snow and hopped onto the porch, where he stamped his shoes and began digging snow out of the tops of them. This opened the gap between shoe and foot, and the snow slid down to his instep. He went inside cursing the day he hadn't been born in Florida. He handed the sack to Foley. "You got any clean glasses?"

Foley got started on Horvath, and it was a question whether Tuttle could get him off the subject, not that he wanted to at first. Leave it to Horvath to reconnoiter. "You took him across in a boat?"

Foley dipped his chin and gave Tuttle the fish eye. "Don't ask."

"Was it a canoe?"

"A canoe! In this weather? You're crazy."

"The marina rents canoes?"

"In the summer, sure. We're the only one on the river that does rent them."

"Oh, there must be some others."

"Nope. They just sit there stacked all week, but they're our big money-maker weekends."

"How does it work?"

"What do you mean, how does it work?"

"I don't know. Say I want to rent a canoe. I don't mean now, take it easy. It's summer and I come in and say, let me have a canoe."

"It'll cost you five bucks the first hour, three each additional hour."

"In advance?"

Foley was warming to the subject, though the brandy, which smelled a bit like paint remover, must have helped.

"You have to deposit twenty-five dollars. Credit cards accepted."

"That's how you guard against theft?"

"What do you mean?"

"If I use a credit card, you know who I am. I don't show up, that twenty-five dollars isn't going to cover the cost of a new canoe, is it?"

"Everybody registers, Tuttle."

"So I write my name and then steal your canoe."

Foley nodded sadly. "We lose a couple every season. A couple canoes."

"You must know who stole them if people register. I suppose you check them off when they come in."

Foley was losing interest. Tuttle twisted the metal cap off the brandy, held it out to Foley and then stopped, struck by a thought.

"I want to see last season's canoe records."

"What the hell for?" Foley's eye was on the bottle.

"Where are they?"

"In the office."

"Get them. When you come back we'll have another drink."

There's nothing more pathetic than a lush. What wouldn't Foley do for a couple more ounces of this cheap brandy? Tuttle shook his head, then decided to have a Sneaky Pete. He splashed brandy into his own glass and tossed it off before Foley got back with the book. Tuttle gave him the bottle in exchange.

System, that was the thing. Mrs. Grice had disappeared in late September. Tuttle turned immediately to that month. Only a page and a half of entries in the ledger, the name printed first by the person in charge, then signed by the one renting the canoe. A check mark and the time of return. There was one entry without a check mark. September 28. The canoe signed out at 10:45 A.M. Tuttle tipped the book so that the page was lit up by Foley's heater. *C. Amore* was the way the name was printed, but the signature did not stop with the initial. Was *Con* a man or a woman, Conrad or Constance? Tuttle was almost filled with awe. By God, he was really onto something.

"I'll put this back," he said to Foley.

Foley only nodded. In the office, Tuttle tore from the ledger the page bearing the name of C. Amore, who had rented a boat and never returned it last September 28. He would just have a little talk with Mr. or Miss Amore, as the case might be.

Except that there was no Amore in any directory in a radius of fifty miles. Lots of D'Amore's and di Amores, but not a single, simple Amore in the bunch.

A setback, no doubt about it, but Tuttle did not lose confidence that he had stumbled onto something important, something that would enable him to lay a plausible claim to Grice's fifty thousand dollars.

He wandered down the hall, opened Horowitz's door and walked in. The private investigator was seated at his computer. He seemed to have a game on the screen, and was engaged in zapping beetlelike objects that wandered erratically over the monitor.

"What do you have to report?" Tuttle asked wearily, claiming a chair.

"Report?"

"On the Grice matter."

"No point in following him. He's in the hospital. Tried to kill himself."

"Say that again. Slowly."

Horowitz obliged. Another setback? For the past hour he had been imagining a stranger paddling off in the canoe. Now he could almost see Arthur Grice himself heading out from the marina.

Had Grice specified that he himself could not be the solution to the mystery of his wife's disappearance, or no fifty thousand? Of course not. As far as Tuttle could see, he was still on Go.

Sixteen

L ooking at Arthur Grice, Cy Horvath felt more certain
than ever that he never wanted his stomach pumped.
Not that he would die first, but he didn't ever want to
be in a position where that desperate remedy was called for.
This being clear, in case anyone was taking note of his wishes,
Cy reflected that Grice had been lucky. Pumped for the wrong
thing, he had nonetheless been saved from death.

During the interview, it had been as much a matter of telling
Grice what had happened as of getting information out of him.
His last memory was of sitting at his desk. The next thing he
knew he awoke with the feeling that a very large animal was
dining on his insides.

"Madeleva found me?"

"You didn't answer when she buzzed you to take a call."

"And she called emergency?"

It was hard to know if he was grateful, angry, or just regis-
tering the facts. Where had the Coke come from?

"I asked for it," he said, as if dredging up memories of his childhood.

"Asked Madeleva?"

"I never drink Coke, but I was chock full of coffee and after the boat house . . . what I felt like was a stiff drink, but I had things to do." A cloud passed over his mind. "I want to talk to Pamela."

"In a minute."

"Lieutenant, I am running a business."

Cy shook his head. "Right now you are in intensive care suspected of committing suicide. That's against the law."

"Crap. How many people have you arrested for attempting suicide?"

"You would be the first."

"You're out of luck, because I didn't do it."

"Then someone tried to kill you."

"With aspirin?"

"No, with arsenic."

Grice had been at his desk, having returned to the office after seeing the dead body of his missing wife, wanting to work because he had to and because it seemed the only way he could get through the turn of events. Uncharacteristically, he'd asked his secretary to bring him a Coke. The next thing he knew, he was in the hospital. That was his story.

In it, Madeleva played the role of lifesaver. But she was also the one who brought him a Coke laced with arsenic.

Horvath let Pamela in to see Grice while he talked with Madeleva. The woman was like a taller, frozen Agnes Lamb.

"You saved his life."

"So he is out of danger?"

"Unless someone slips him another Coke."

"I brought him that."

"Tell me about it."

She hesitated, but she would have had time to think about it anyway. When she spoke her voice was the same as always.

"Mr. Grice has a motto. Do It Yourself. He does not follow his own advice, but he often says that. Do it yourself. I wish I had."

"You sent someone else for the Coke?"

"Yes."

There was a bar in Grice's office, seldom used, and she had not noticed it contained no soda pop. Mr. Grice never drank it, but there were clients who would ask for it when offered a drink. The Coke machines were at the far end of the building, in the employee lunch-room. She had sent Walsh the security guard for it.

"You will think I could have poisoned the drink after Mr. Walsh brought it."

"Did you?"

"No."

"Did he?"

"Someone did."

Walsh? Once more Cy had the feeling that what had seemed clear-cut was dissolving into confusion. Go back to the beginning. Arthur Grice was in the hospital as an attempted suicide. Whether Walsh or Madeleva brought him the Coke was less important than that he had drunk enough arsenic to kill him twice. If it was self-administered, right after the discovery of his wife's death, suicide could be explained as either despairing grief or guilty fear that he would be found out.

Madeleva went into her boss's room and while he waited for Pamela to come out, Cy reflected on the implausibility of Grice committing suicide because he was responsible for his wife's death. If he had killed her, it was unlikely he would have put her in a canoe and sunk it in his own boat house. And what about the obliging anonymous telephone calls that had sent them first to the roadside, where they'd found the shoe, and then to the boat house, where they'd found its match? But one of the shoes had been under water and ice for some time, perhaps since the end of September. The other did not even show the effects of being out on a roadside in winter weather. It didn't make a lot of sense that Grice would be both the killer and the caller. But the caller knew too much to be simply passing on randomly collected facts.

Maybe Arthur Grice had attempted suicide out of remorse for killing his wife, but Cy Horvath would not want the task of convincing the prosecutor's office of that. Maybe Arthur Grice had attempted suicide out of simple grief at the death of his wife. But the caller seemed intent on directing suspicion toward Grice.

If, on the other hand, an attempt had been made on Grice's life by putting arsenic in his Coke, it had to have been done by someone in the offices of Grice Enterprises. It was beginning to look like talking with Walsh was more urgent than Cy wanted to think.

Horvath looked into Grice's room. The now pale and haggard entrepreneur, as of just a few hours ago a certified widower, lay on his back talking with Pamela Mathers, who stood at the side of the bed. On the other side, toward the foot of the bed, Madeleva followed the conversation impassively. Horvath was surprised to overhear that the topic was a massive new venture under Pamela's direction, involving a chain of rental video stores. Not exactly a wake.

"How come there was an empty aspirin bottle lying on your desk?"

The three of them stared at him as if he were nuts. Grice answered. "Because I had just taken the last one in the bottle with my Coke."

"That explains that."

Horvath's offer to take either or both of the women back to Grice Enterprises was accepted by Madeleva. Pamela had her Cherokee; besides, she wasn't ready to go.

"You will talk with Mr. Walsh?" Madeleva asked when they were on their way. More snow was beginning to fall, and the monotonous rhythm of the windshield wipers filled the car.

"Yes. I don't expect much to come of it."

She said nothing. Cy was not much of a talker, but he had met his match in Madeleva. The woman obviously had no intention of volunteering a thing. He found that he had no desire to fill the silence with chatter. He had the feeling that she was as conscious of his silence as he was of hers.

Walsh did not see them come in. He stood looking out a window at the snow, a cigarette cupped in one of the hands joined behind him. Madeleva went on to her office. Cy stood next to Walsh.

"I want you to reconstruct for me, step by step, getting that Coke for Grice."

Walsh jumped in surprise, then stared pop-eyed at Horvath. "God damn it, it's not funny sneaking up on someone like that."

"I thought you were on duty."

"I am on duty."

"Can we stipulate that you were notified of your rights, or do you want me to read Miranda to you?"

"What the hell are you talking about?"

"Your attempt to kill Grice with a poisoned drink."

"You're drunk."

"Show me the employees' lunchroom, will you, Walsh? I want to see the machine from which you bought that Coke for Grice."

Walsh finally seemed to figure out what Cy was talking about. "You want to see the lunchroom?"

"If that's where you went to get the Coke for Mr. Grice."

"That's where it came from." Walsh looked at the cigarette he held, then took one more drag before burying it in the sand of a receptacle.

Cy thought about Walsh's answer. Was he being coy? "Did you personally go get that Coke for Grice?"

"I didn't have to."

"Why not?"

"Miss Mathers brought it for me. She was going to get one for herself and saved me the trip."

"Pamela Mathers brought the Coke from the lunchroom and gave it to you?"

"And I gave it to Madeleva."

"I believe you."

"Thank you all to hell." But Walsh was obviously pleased to be treated as a colleague again.

"You've been a big help and I appreciate it."

Walsh shrugged. "We're in the same profession still, Horvath."

"Pamela Mathers handed you a Coke, which you then handed to Madeleva?"

"Right."

"Where were you when you took the cup from Pamela?"

"You mean exactly?"

"If you remember."

Walsh smiled as if he were constantly being assailed by memories, large and small. He limped pigeon-toed across the great expanse of the reception area to a corridor. He stopped just inside the reception area. "Here."

"How far to the lunchroom?"

Walsh set off again, down the corridor, and Horvath followed. They had not got far when they came to a door bearing Pamela Mather's name.

Cy stepped inside and closed the door. It was a room perhaps twenty feet by twelve, without windows, which, compared with the reception area and Grice's office, was small. The desk faced the door, and behind it was a table on which a computer stood. There were file cabinets, and a bookshelf that seemed to contain nothing but computer manuals. In one corner was a TV set with a VCR and a stack of videotapes.

Cy went behind the desk and opened the middle drawer, bending over to study its contents but leaving them undisturbed. He opened the top right desk drawer and there it was. A bottle of arsenic. The doorknob was turning slowly. Horvath waited. The door opened a crack and then was pushed in. Walsh said, "What're you doing in here? I thought you wanted to see the goddamn lunchroom."

"Come here."

"What for?"

"I am searching this desk and I want you as a witness."

"Damn it, Horvath, I work here. My job is to ask you what the hell you're doing."

Cy opened the right-hand top drawer again.

"Ah! What have we here?"

Using his handkerchief he removed the bottle and held it up. "A bottle of arsenic."

"Poison?"

"The same kind found in Grice's Coke."

"How do I know you didn't put it there?"

"There is a better question."

"Yeah?"

"How do I know you didn't plant it there, Walsh?"

"Horvath, do me a favor. Go to hell."

Cy wrapped the bottle in his handkerchief and put it in his pocket.

"I'll give you a receipt for this."

Walsh made an obscene suggestion as to where Cy could put his receipt and left the room. Cy picked up the phone and placed a call to Phil Keegan.

Seventeen

rthur indicated he wanted her to stay at the hospital with him when Madeleva returned to the office with Lieutenant Horvath.

"Close the door, Pam."

The policeman on duty outside shook his head when she began to shut the door. Pam looked back toward Arthur.

"They want it to stay open."

He nodded, his eyes fixed on the ceiling. She returned to the side of the bed. "Someone tried to kill me."

"Why?"

His eyes moved from the ceiling to her. "Why did they want to kill Frankie?"

It wasn't a question but an expression of wonder. He shook his head slowly from side to side. "Think of it. For all these months she was down there in the boat house."

His eyes filled with tears, which overflowed and ran down the side of his face. Pam's own eyes misted. Seeing a man cry removed a major prop of the universe. What bunk it was to want men to be as emotional as women. But at the limit men cried too, and it was the realization that their tears were signs of helplessness, of confusion, of being overwhelmed, that frightened her. Pam had never known Arthur not to be in control. He was the most manly man she had ever known, light-years away from her lovers. Maybe that was why she thought of him as a father or a brother, as a symbol of strength. To be treated as an equal by such a man was a genuine tribute. And now he lay on a hospital bed weeping because his wife was dead and an attempt had been made on his own life, and she didn't blame him.

"You haven't any enemies," she said.

He smiled and blinked his eyes dry. "I've got lots of enemies. Everytime you win a bid, you make enemies." He released a little laugh. "Every time you do someone a favor you make an enemy."

"No one has any reason to kill you."

"I wish you were right."

"Do you know who it might be?"

A fleeting look of anguish crossed his features. "I honest to God don't. They got Frankie and they tried to get me. I suppose they'll try again."

"There's a policeman outside."

"Check his ID." He added quickly, "I'm kidding. I'm glad he's there. Did Father Dowling go?"

"I think so. Would you like to see him?"

"If he comes back."

When she was outside, behind the wheel of her Cherokee, it struck Pam that it was Arthur's question about Father Dowling that had been his reason for asking her to stay. The conversation with Father Dowling seemed to suggest he was thinking the same thing. The priest was there in case Arthur wanted him, and Arthur was willing to see the priest if he came to the hospital. Pam decided to do something about it.

The trouble was that she was moving into an unknown area.

Religion had never been part of her life, as a kid or at any time since. What she knew of it, she didn't like. She had the vague sense that it was something surpassed by science and by everything. Didn't psychology explain what people were looking for when they believed in God and said their prayers? The fear of death was at the bottom of it.

Was the fear of death an explanation or something to be explained? It didn't seem like something you could get over, as if it didn't matter to you. Pam had never given much thought to death, but now with Frankie definitely dead and Arthur in intensive care, it no longer seemed remote. Still, she knew it would become remote again, as the death of her parents had. Then she had felt betrayed and abandoned. What right did they have to get killed in a plane crash and leave her alone at thirteen? It wasn't fair. Even now when she thought of her parents, which was rarely, it was difficult to keep resentment from her mind. Besides, nowadays everybody seemed to be talking about life after death, reincarnation, transmigration. It wasn't exactly religion, maybe, but it sure wasn't science.

When she parked and came through the basement to the elevator, Conway lowered his paper and looked at her. What a creep.

There was no entry for *Dowling, Roger* in the telephone directory. Pam felt stymied. Surely he must have a phone. If it was in the name of his church, she would have to know the name, but she didn't. She decided to call Captain Keegan, who seemed to know the priest pretty well.

"I was just thinking of you," Keegan said.

"Oh."

"I wonder if we could talk."

"Sure."

"Are you at your office?"

"No. I'm home. But first tell me something. How can I get in touch with the priest who was at the hospital with you? Father Dowling."

"Give him a call."

"He's not in the book."

"It's St. Hilary's parish. I'll give you the number." He did, and she thanked him.

The phone was answered almost immediately, by a woman, which surprised Pamela.

"Could I speak to Father Dowling?"

"Who's calling, please?"

"Pamela Mathers."

"One moment." Something in the woman's voice suggested she recognized the name.

"Roger Dowling here. Pamela?"

"This is kind of an odd request but I feel I should make it. I think Arthur Grice would like to talk with you. He didn't ask me to call you, but I think he wanted me to."

"He hasn't had a relapse, has he?"

"Oh, no. He's okay. Physically. But his wife's death has finally hit and then he realized someone tried to kill him too."

"Is that certain?"

"There was poison in his drink and he didn't put it there."

"Well, of course I'll go see him."

After she hung up the phone, Pamela envied Arthur having someone to talk to. Since Frankie had disappeared, she had often filled that role for him. She smiled.

Pam had done drugs, had sex as if it were no more than a handshake, and shared her apartment twice, once with the idea that it might lead to something permanent. Two twits, as it turned out. Guys who talked like the men in prime-time comedies, with nothing between their ears. One had thought of lovemaking as an art form, and the other was disturbingly passive. If it hadn't been for her slide rule and her pocket calculator, Pam would have lost her mind. The happiest day of her life was the day Harold moved out. He cried when they embraced for the last time, but she would bet he had forgotten their seven and a half months of cohabitation by the time he his car was in gear.

Work had saved her, just as demanding courses had helped her survive the drug scene as an undergraduate. Arthur Grice created a new position for her after she proved herself on the Aurora Mall and the Barrington Civic Center. When she wasn't supervising ongoing projects, she was helping Arthur put together bids on future jobs. Her suggestion that they dominate the rental video market in the northern and western suburbs intrigued him. With the sanity-threatening disappearance of Frankie, he had needed the therapy of a daring but potentially very rewarding effort.

They had spent more time together than she had spent with her live-ins, but it had been straight-up business and no nonsense, with not even the suggestion that the thought had crossed his mind. She sometimes wondered what her reaction would be if he ever did make a move.

He was a man. He was decades older than she was. He was enormously successful, had vast and variegated experience, yet he talked with her as an equal, and respected her mind with no condescension. When he disagreed with her it was on a basis she could respect. And of course she knew about the rumors.

When she *was* messing around, no one cared or seemed to notice much, but now when there was zilch the rumors flew, and she would have done anything to stop them. But she couldn't very well run an ad in the company newsletter announcing that she was not sleeping with Arthur Grice. The ugly aspect of the rumors was what they suggested about Frankie's disappearance.

Pam liked to dream of Frankie showing up one day, hale and hearty, with a perfectly plausible explanation of her absence. She even went into an Albanian Orthodox church in Chicago and lit a candle for Frankie's safe return. Arthur just looked at her when she told him that, then turned away.

"Are you Catholic?" he asked over his shoulder.

"I'm not even Albanian."

He liked that about her, unexpected answers, and it worked then as it had before. He had half a grin when he turned around.

"Maybe it'll work. The police are getting nowhere."

She had known the kind of questions he was asked, and then the newspapers became vicious. At first Arthur had been the tragic husband, mystified by his wife's disappearance. But writers grew bored with that, and on the basis of guesses began talking about a killing. Of course then, they needed a killer. And a motive. That's where she had come in. Because Arthur had stayed overnight in her apartment.

It had happened twice. They had been working, he'd stretched out on the couch to take forty winks and had slept through the night. Pamela hadn't given it a second thought, except to be glad he was getting the rest. The second time she gave him her bed and went downstairs to Judy McFarland's apartment, which was empty since Judy was on a Rome flight with TWA that month.

When Arthur hired Horowitz, Pam was astounded. Duke had done security work on job sites for them, and Arthur had to know the man was no whiz.

"Of course he's a joke, Pam. If the thought of Horowitz as competition doesn't stir up the police, I don't know what will."

Pamela acted as liaison with Horowitz, and as a test she gave him the number of her Cherokee. She could shake him within minutes, but the car driven by the big guy who had to be a cop was something else. Every time she thought she had lost him, he would show up again. The spinout on the Mannheim Road gave her the chance to see him up close. He could have been a lineman for the Bears. He didn't pretend not to be a cop, and Pamela began to think of Lieutenant Horvath as her police escort. Now that Frankie was dead and Arthur in the hospital, she liked even better the thought that Horvath was looking out for her. She imagined she could talk with him. But that was silly.

The only other person she could think of to call was Madeleva. She phoned work and asked Madeleva to stop by later. Madeleva agreed without surprise, delight, or any emotion. After she hung up, Pam wondered if she had made a mistake. It wouldn't be necessary to explain to Madeleva what was going on, which was an advantage, but the woman certainly wasn't a barrel of laughs. Maybe she would loosen up after a drink.

Because of the snow and the condition of the street outside, she told Madeleva to drive into the basement garage. "Tell the man to give me a ring and I'll come down."

"Oh, I'll find a parking spot outside."

"It's snowing again."

"That's all right. What's the address again?"

Eighteen

lthough *Amore* did not appear in any directories of the Chicago area, Tuttle did not despair. He knew he was onto something and patience was his ally. At stake was fifty thousand dollars, and it was a delicate task to try to find out things without tipping his mitt. He didn't want anyone cutting himself in as partner to this deal.

Which is why he was keeping his distance from Duke Horowitz. He would have to get the rubber check back before reactivating his account and depositing any reward money.

He felt that confident. His confidence did not waver when Peanuts frowned and shook his head when asked if he had ever heard of anyone named Amore. He didn't even ask why he should know the name.

So Tuttle went back to the marina. The watchman did not appreciate being disturbed two days in a row.

"Foley, listen, you watch the news on that thing once in a while don't you?" He flapped a dismissive hand at the television set. "You realize what was discovered in the Grice boat house just across the river, don't you?"

"I told you I was in on it."

"The murder?"

"Ha. I took Horvath over there when they found her."

"Found her in a canoe, Foley."

"I heard about it."

"A canoe from this marina," Tuttle went on, speaking solemnly. "Remember your missing canoes?"

"She never rented any canoe from here that I'm aware of."

"Only you and I know where that canoe came from."

"*I* don't know. Believe me, if she wanted a canoe she could afford to buy one. Not that I see her dying for a canoe."

"In a canoe, Foley, not for one. Sooner or later the connection will be made between the canoe and this marina."

"I don't want cops swarming around here," Foley whined.

"Of course you don't. We have to beat them to the punch."

"Tell me how." Foley's was the voice of despair.

"I know who killed Mrs. Frances Grice, Foley."

"Who?"

"The man who rented the canoe."

"That helps."

"I also know his name. I need your help, Foley. Who is C. Amore?"

"Seymour?"

"*A-m-o-r-e*. Initial *C*."

"The name in the ledger," Foley said. He repeated it, wrestling himself to his feet.

"What are you doing?"

Foley waddled into the office and in a moment came back, carrying the ledger.

He lowered himself into his chair. When he was settled, the dog returned its muzzle to the carpet. Foley began to page through the book.

"What month we talking about?"

"Try July."

But Foley was turning pages back and forth. He glared up at Tuttle. "All right, Tuttle, where is it? A page has been ripped out of here."

Tuttle bounded to Foley's side. "Stolen? My God. What else is missing?"

"Tuttle, the last entry is in August and then there's a page missing."

"The thief was obviously in a hurry. But I think we should check the office anyway. You start on that, I'll call the police . . ."

"Stop," Foley yelped and his dog raised its head as if to bark. "I don't want the police here."

"I don't blame you."

"What's that supposed to mean?"

"Did you report the missing canoe?"

"No!"

"If you had, a woman might be alive today. Who is C. Amore?"

Foley shook his head.

"Who is Con Amore?"

"I don't know."

"He is the murderer, Foley."

This visit was an obvious waste of time. Tuttle decided to cut his losses by leaving. He had trouble starting his car and was visited by the horrible thought of spending the winter at the marina with Foley and his dog. Given the rotten state of his credit, it was doubtful he could get a wrecker to come out here and give him a quick charge. Which was what he was going to need if the damned motor didn't start. And then it did, and Tuttle let out a roaring cheer.

Foley stood in the open door of the marina shack, drawn by the sound of the grinding starter. He joined his hands above his head at the sound of Tuttle's cheer.

Tuttle backed out of there, shifted to drive and was on his

way. Now that he had half let the cat out of the bag he intended to act. He would not put off any longer claiming that fifty thousand dollar reward.

Irish tweed hat in hand, an agonized expression on his face, Tuttle hurried across the reception area of the hospital toward the elevators. His back prickled with apprehension, but no one shouted at him before he ducked into an elevator.

He got off at four, went immediately to the nurses station, and asked what room Mr. Grice was in.

"Mr. Grice?"

"Arthur Grice."

"Sir, this is maternity."

Tuttle slapped himself on the forehead. "Dummy." He stared abjectly at the nurse, whose eyeliner looked as though it had been applied left-handed. "I'm so darn worried I didn't get it right. Could you find out what room Arthur Grice is in?"

When he emerged from the elevator again, he caught sight of Peanuts sitting on a chair outside a room. What luck! Tuttle waved both arms to get Peanuts's attention and then crooked his finger. Peanuts glowered. Tuttle gesticulated frantically, and Peanuts rose to his feet and lumbered toward him.

"I thought you was giving me the finger."

"An old friend like you? Peanuts! Is that the room Arthur Grice is in?"

"I told you. He tried to kill himself. That's why I'm guarding him."

"I won't be long, Peanuts."

"You can't go in there."

"I am a lawyer."

"So what?"

Tuttle leaned toward his friend. "Peanuts, I am that close to fifty thousand dollars." He held up thumb and forefinger, not quite touching. "I know you won't keep me from that."

Peanuts took it under advisement. After a moment, he said, "Five minutes and I didn't see you go in."

Arthur Grice lay on his back, eyes closed, hands folded over his chest. A lily would have completed the picture. Tuttle, hat in hand, cleared his throat. A frown formed on Grice's forehead but he did not open his eyes. Tuttle gave the bed a good bump. Grice woke up and looked at Tuttle.

"Mr. Grice?"

"Who are you?"

"Tuttle. I am a lawyer in Fox River. I'm here to lay claim to the fifty thousand dollar reward."

"What!"

"For information leading to the discovery of your wife . . ."

Grice was on his elbows, glaring at Tuttle. "Get the hell out of here!"

Tuttle turned. Peanuts was peering around the door. Tuttle waved him off.

Grice said, "My wife has already been discovered, you lousy son of a bitch."

"And I know who killed her."

Grice calmed down. He eased himself back on the bed, his eyes never leaving Tuttle's. "Who?"

"You have offered a fifty thousand dollar reward for information leading to the apprehension of her killer?"

"Yes!"

"The offer is still in force?"

"If you help find the man who killed my wife I will give you fifty thousand dollars."

Tuttle pulled up a chair.

Grice said, "Tell me first, then tell the police."

"As an officer of the court, I could scarcely do otherwise."

"Who did it?"

"The man who rented the canoe in which she was found."

"It was rented?"

"From the marina on the bank opposite your boat house."

"Who rented it?"

"Do you know a man named Amore?"

Grice thought about it, his eyes fixed on Tuttle, his lower lip protruding. He shook his head slowly.

"C. Amore."

"No."

Tuttle shifted on the chair. "Maybe this will help." He leaned toward Grice. "Con Amore."

Grice sat upright like Lazarus. "What!"

"Con Amore."

Grice tried to grab him, but Tuttle pushed back, overturning the chair that fell with a crash. Peanuts came into the room. Grice was trying to get out of bed.

"Arrest that man, officer."

Tuttle sidled past Peanuts into the hall. Behind them, Grice's shouting grew louder. Tuttle scampered to the stairway and pulled open the heavy door. Peanuts, gripping his sleeve, had come along.

"That man is psycho, Peanuts. I would keep a close eye on him."

He pulled free and went thundering down the stairwell.

Nineteen

Cy Horvath was playing a hunch, which was why he had not yet called in about what he had found in Pamela Mathers's desk. He sat in a straight-back chair in a utility room in the executive corridor at Grice Enterprises. His hunch was that she would be returning to her office, and he liked the idea of bringing her *and* the bottle of arsenic downtown to Keegan.

What had happened seemed pretty clear. She had gone for the Coke, brought it to her office, doctored it, then given the drink to Walsh.

Walsh was scared skinny by the thought that he had brought his boss a lethal drink, which was why he had not objected to Cy's ploy. He had let him into the room across from Pamela's and had left the door open a crack, so the door of Pamela's office was visible. Cy had returned the bottle to the desk drawer. He would bet a significant sum on the probability that she would be coming back to get rid of that bottle.

He sat in the darkened room like a priest in his confessional, except that Cy was interested in capturing a sinner, not forgiving one. What Pamela's motive was in trying to poison her boss Cy did not know. Nor did he ask himself if the woman who had tried to kill the husband was responsible for the death of the wife. If no such parlay was in the offing, Pamela was not likely to face any large troubles. Given the timid souls in the prosecuting office, she might even escape indictment. A mere murder attempt did not loom large on the prosecutor's scales.

Such thoughts were not conducive to peace of mind as Cy sat there in the dark, the sliver of light admitted by the slight opening almost painfully bright. What cop would throw himself into any case if he wasted time calculating the odds of the criminal getting the punishment he deserved? The only way to handle it was to consider the cops' job one thing, and the court's another. Connected, maybe; if the cops did their job right, nothing that happened later in court could undo it.

Whenever he heard footsteps Cy pulled the door toward him, not closing it entirely. He had been there half an hour when steps approached and he pulled the door to. The steps came to a halt across the hall. Cy eased his door open.

She was just disappearing into her office, one flashing calf, one high heel, and the door closed. Cy rose, went into the hall, paused a moment to ready himself, and the door opened again. Madeleva looked out at him. Her eyes widened slightly.

"Miss Mathers is not coming back this afternoon."

"I'd hoped to see her."

"I'll get the message to her."

"Thank you."

On his way out, he walked past Walsh without looking at him. He sat in his car in the employee parking lot and felt like a damned fool. It could have been a lot worse. What if he had barged in and found the wrong woman in the office? Jeez. Now the bottle was in the desk and he would have to go back for it. And he did not want to run into Madeleva again. He felt enough of a fool as it was.

Some minutes later he saw the stately secretary come out of the building. She wore a long, dark fur coat and a matching fur cap. Stylish but cold, she hurried toward the lot, unlocked the door of a green BMW, and slipped in behind the wheel. This was a break. He would wait till she left, then go in for the bottle of arsenic.

Madeleva drove off, gunning the motor and spinning the wheels. Her driving character seemed different from her lofty demeanor when not on wheels. Cy got out of his car and trotted toward the entrance, his open coat flapping around him.

"Did Madeleva catch you in the closet?" Walsh asked in school-yard tones.

Cy stopped. "What did she say?"

"Madeleva? Nothing."

Cy went on to Pamela's office, let himself in, went behind the desk, and opened the drawer. He sat down and looked deeper into it. Frowning, he tried the other drawers, not really believing he could have been mistaken. He went back to the top right drawer and began to pile its contents on top of the desk. A futile task. The bottle was missing.

He sat back and suddenly realized what that meant.

Madeleva.

His impulse was to get up, run out, and drive off in the hope of finding her. He stayed calm. Among the books lying on the table behind the desk was a directory of Grice Enterprises employees. It took him a moment to find it. He had forgotten the last name, but the distinctive first name made it easy. Madeleva Haimu. He put the book in his pocket, and once more walked past Walsh without looking at him.

Thank God he hadn't reported in about finding the poison. But thinking that made him feel worse. He had made an unforgivable mistake and did not intend to conceal it. But first he was going to do everything he could to rectify it.

Madeleva's address was a town house in a development that had been put up by Grice Enterprises. The development was in the shape of a figure eight around an artificial lake at one end and an Olympic-size swimming pool at the other. From the gate house, Cy could see just outside the cyclone fence that enclosed the pool an elegant maintenance building with, inevitably, a mansard roof. There was a guard at the gate. During the last couple of days, Cy was getting a vivid idea what happened to cops when they retired. This one was named Histon.

"Normally we keep the visitor's driver's license while he's in the compound."

"You want mine?"

"Forget it."

"Do you know Madeleva Haimu?"

"Town house 17A."

"Did she just drive through here?"

Histon shook his head. "You mean recently?"

"Within the last fifteen minutes."

"No. Definitely not."

"No need for me to go in, then. I'll just back out."

"Any message for her?"

Cy put on the brakes and eased back to the gate house. "No message. Understand?"

Histon agreed that there was no message. Cy backed out, went down the street, turned and came back and parked where he could see any car that turned in at the development. After fifteen minutes his feeling that he was making a fool of himself increased. If she had been coming home she would have been here long ago. She could have stopped to shop, she could have had an accident, all kinds of things might have happened to explain the fact that she was not here, but Cy did not believe any of them.

And then he thought of Pamela Mathers. Madeleva had gone to her office. She knew that Pamela was not returning. Had Pamela called and asked her to bring the bottle in her desk? He had left the motor running. He put the car in gear and took off.

He pulled into the driveway and pressed the horn. Soon the

doors lifted, and he dipped down into the brightly lit basement garage. He continued and didn't stop until he could see a pop-eyed Conway looking out of his little office as if he feared the car was coming right on through. The hood gave Conway a little curtsy when Cy hit the brakes. He turned off the engine and hopped out.

"Good afternoon, Lieutenant."

"What floor is Pamela Mathers on?"

"Still after that, are you?" Conway said, leering. "Miz Mathers is on four."

"She up there?"

"That's her Jeep right over there."

"She have visitors?"

"Now, Lieutenant, I don't pry into the private lives of either tenants or lieutenants."

Someday Cy would like to pop Conroy in the mouth, but today was not the day. He entered the elevator and punched four. The car rose very slowly. When it reached the fourth floor, it seemed to settle into itself a bit before the door slid open.

He rapped authoritatively on Pamela's door and, impatient, rapped again while the echo of the first was still in the hallway. He knocked four times in the space of a minute, then lowered his shoulder and banged the door open.

The living room was empty. "Miss Mathers," Cy called, coming on through.

She was in the kitchen, slumped to the floor from the chair in which she had been sitting. There was a cup of tea on the table before her. Keegan grabbed the wall phone and dialed emergency.

He gave the address of the building and of the apartment. "I think it's a poisoning. Arsenic. Should I do anything?"

In peripheral vision he saw a movement, but before he had realized it was an angled reflection in the dining-room mirror, it was gone. Someone had been in the apartment. He was receiving instructions on what to do while he waited for the paramedics.

There was no way he could abandon Pamela Mathers and see who had just left the apartment. Not that it mattered. He was morally certain it had been Madeleva Haimu.

Twenty

It seemed that he was always either burying people or visiting them in hospitals. Arthur Grice had been released from the hospital, but Pamela Mathers had taken his place. Both had been poisoned, it seemed, by the same hand.

"Grice's secretary," Phil Keegan said. "A very beautiful woman. Black. I had Agnes arrest her thinking it was a favor, but of course she found some racist motive in it. Maybe she's right."

Madeleva had been arrested and booked. There seemed little doubt that she would be indicted for the attempted murder of two of her superiors at Grice Enterprises.

"But why?"

"Jealousy. Apparently with the wife out of the way, she expected a clear track with Grice, and Pamela was getting in the way."

"But why poison Grice?"

"If she ever talks maybe she can explain it."

Madeleva had said nothing since her arrest, and as far as Phil could see she'd never speak again. Because she was a woman, he reasoned, she was irrational, and because she was black she was inscrutable.

"Roger, that is a combination that defies understanding."

"You think she killed the wife as well?"

"We're looking into it."

If Arthur Grice had commissioned Pamela to invite Roger Dowling to talk to him, this new turn of events had changed his mind. The priest found the entrepreneur distant on personal matters and genuinely baffled by Madeleva's deeds.

Pamela remembered making tea for herself and Madeleva when the secretary came by her apartment, and that was that. Until the hospital.

"I think I prefer poison to the remedy," she said to Roger Dowling.

"Thank God you're alive."

She smiled, but soon it faded. "I always thought Madeleva and I got along so well. What will happen to her?"

"I'm no lawyer."

"If she read and believed those newspaper stories, I can understand why she would hate me. But she should have known they were false. But Arthur! What was the point of trying to kill him?"

"Each man kills the thing he loves."

"Is that the Mills Brothers?"

"Oscar Wilde. How would you know about the Mills Brothers?"

"I bought the tapes of a golden oldie station that was switching to rock. Who's Oscar Wilde?"

"A poet."

"Never heard of him."

"He wouldn't have liked that."

"What he said is true, isn't it? We do more harm to those we love than to those we hate."

Arthur Grice came when Roger was still there. He looked

around the room. "It's amazing how different this place looks when you're a visitor."

"Have you seen Madeleva?"

His brow darkened. "What for?"

"Don't you want to ask her why?"

"What difference does it make?" But Arthur wore the slightly bewildered look of a man a woman had loved enough to want to kill.

"Maybe you're right."

"The one good thing about it is that now I understand what has been happening."

Roger said, "You mean to your wife?"

"Don't ask me how she did it, but there's no other explanation."

He told Phil that he had had no idea that Madeleva regarded him as anything other than her boss. They had never done anything social together, before or after the disappearance of his wife. The woman had given no sign of the jealousy that was supposedly her motive. Not that Arthur Grice doubted it. He was almost eager to accept this dispelling of the mystery that had enveloped him in recent months.

"Will you bury my wife, Father?" Grice asked this when they had stepped into the hall to be out of the way of the nurses tending to Pamela.

"Was she a Catholic?"

"We were both raised Catholic."

"You don't have a parish?"

"Saint Hilary's was my family's parish."

"Of course I will. Have you chosen a funeral director?"

"McDivitt. He suggested you but I had made up my mind to ask you."

"Stop by the rectory today or tomorrow and we'll get it all settled."

"I haven't been in the neighborhood for a long time. I went to grade school there. Is the school still standing?"

"It's now a parish center. We have programs for the retired and for what are called senior citizens."

"I'd like to go see the school while I'm out there." He rubbed his chin with a large hand. "Do you know what I keep thinking? I could be dead now."

"An unsettling thought."

"What's really unsettling is that it's been true all along. Now I know it."

Arthur Grice had not mentioned Tuttle but Roger had the story from Keegan.

"Roger, you remember the ring and its inscription?"

"Yes."

"From AG to FG. *Con amore.* Anyway, just when I hear that Tuttle is trying to shake Grice down on his sickbed, a call comes from a guy named Foley, who works at a marina across from the Grices. He wants to report a missing canoe. He insists on speaking to me. He thinks a canoe stolen from the marina provided Mrs. Grice's final transportation. He was right. He then says the canoe was rented by a man named Amore. Con Amore. I had just been talking with Grice. The same as in the ring. So we are back to playing games."

"It doesn't sound like Madeleva."

"You got a better suggestion?"

"Me?"

Roger certainly wished he did. Later he stood at his study window and watched Forbes clearing snow from the walkways, snow that just kept falling. Phil called what was happening games, but they were played with serious intent. Roger Dowling had great difficulty seeing Grice's secretary behind all this, although he had never met her. Only an incoherent image formed itself in his mind as people spoke of her. Phil seemed not to see it all as a bewildering series of events that had started emphatically at St. Hilary with Father Don's magic show. Roger Dowling did find it difficult to believe that

Madeleva had killed one person and sought to kill two more, but even if she had, it would not explain everything. What about Aggie Miller?

Here Roger Dowling felt he was on solid ground. Any unified theory of the recent violent deaths had to include that of Aggie Miller. And this meant whoever killed Aggie knew she had the ring with the telltale inscription. And in order to know that, the killer would have to have been present at the magic show, or have obtained the information from someone who had been there. Surely that ruled out Madeleva.

Phil's response to this was that the investigation was only beginning. He proclaimed that he would bet his bottom dollar that all these recent deaths were interconnected.

Maybe so.

Twenty-One

When Arthur Grice told him about Tuttle's visit to the hospital, Keegan sent Cy to haul in the little lawyer for questioning. That turned out to be easier said than done. Apparently Peanuts Pianone had been the last one to see Tuttle, and that was only a view of his backside as he lit down the stairway after waving the red flag in Grice's face.

"I'll tell you one thing, though," Grice said. "Once I got out of bed to go after that son of a bitch I never got into it again. I had had too much hospital and didn't know it."

"You say he quoted the inscription of the ring?"

"That's right. You still have it, don't you?"

Keegan nodded. "Aggie Miller's daughter plans to make a legal claim on it, but for the moment it remains in our custody."

"That ring belongs to me!"

"Did Tuttle mention the ring?"

"Captain, I don't know what his game was. It was as if he

· 130 ·

came to see me only to taunt me. He said he knew who killed my wife."

"What's that got to do with the ring?"

"He said the killer's name was Con Amore." Grice shook his head. "Con Amore rented a canoe and killed my wife, that was the message. He's lucky I didn't get my hands on him."

It looked as if anyone would be lucky to lay hands on Tuttle. The little lawyer had disappeared.

"Maybe he'll show up in a sunken canoe, too."

Keegan leaned forward and kissed Agnes on the forehead. "Thank you."

"What's that for?"

"For pointing out where we can find Tuttle. Come on, Cy."

"Can't I come along?" Agnes asked sarcastically.

"If you ride in the backseat."

But she was not to be put off by teasing. When they got to the garage, Phil told Agnes to drive and got into the backseat himself.

"I always wanted a chauffeur."

"Buckle up. Where are we going?"

"To the marina."

The snow had stopped falling the day before, the sun was out and some melting had begun. Icicles hung from the eaves of the marina building and sparkled in the sunlight. After they had parked, Agnes stayed in the car as lookout, Cy waded through the soggy snow to the river side of the building, and Phil went up to the door and pounded on it. Very hard. Hard enough to start a dog inside bellowing.

"Foley!" Keegan shouted. "Open up. Police."

"I got a cold," Foley said when he peered red-eyed over the still-connected door chain. He sniffled and applied a Kleenex to his nose. "What can I do for you?"

"Let me in."

Foley sneezed, coughed, and searched the pocket of his coat sweater for another Kleenex. "I ought to be quarantined."

"Open up or I'm coming in by force."

"You got a warrant?"

"Do I need a warrant to talk to a colleague?"

This appeal to Foley's residual pride in his job helped. Leaning on the door until the chain snapped helped too. Keegan pushed Foley aside and made a rapid survey of the interior.

"You alone?"

"The marina's closed, Keegan."

"Tell me about the stolen canoe you reported."

"I'm sorry I called."

"When did you last see Tuttle?"

Foley could not look him in the eye when he said, "Tuttle? Why the hell would I see Tuttle?"

"Because you're going to need a lawyer if you don't stop playing games. Tuttle is a fugitive from the law." Keegan raised his voice as he said this. "When I catch that son of a bitch, not only will he never practice law again, he is going to spend a very long time as guest of the government."

"Why are you shouting?"

"To make sure I'm heard."

"I'm not deaf."

"How about the dog?"

The dog's ears had lifted and were pointing toward the office. Keegan had checked the office quickly when he'd come in, but now he began to move slowly toward it, watching Foley's face. There was no doubt about it. He was getting warm.

"Tuttle was in on the Mrs. Grice murder, that much is certain. God knows what else he's involved in."

Keegan stepped into the office and looked around. The desk chair was shoved back against the far wall. Keegan went around the desk and leaned over to look into the knee well.

"Come on out, Tuttle."

"Is that you, Captain Keegan? Thank God!"

The little lawyer, his tweed hat sideways on his head, backed out and stood, thrusting his hand at Keegan. "Captain, I'm fearful for my life."

"I'm not surprised."

"Arthur Grice threatened to kill me."

"I don't blame him."

Keegan escorted Tuttle into the room where Foley had collapsed into a chair.

"You got him," Foley said, sighing with relief. "He threatened me."

Tuttle shook his head and smiled sadly at Keegan. "Strange what an overheated room will do to the human mind."

"He's the one who ripped the page out of the ledger," Foley yelped. For some reason the dog began to bark.

"Protective custody," Tuttle said loftily, pressing a crumpled sheet into Keegan's hand.

Keegan unfolded the ledger page. *C. Amore* was printed in ballpoint and then there was a signature that, sure enough, read *Con Amore.*

"There's your murderer," Tuttle announced. "And Grice owes me fifty thousand dollars whether he likes it or not."

"You think Con Amore is a man?"

Tuttle paused. "Man or woman, what's the difference, the reward is rightly mine."

"It's not a name, Tuttle. It's a phrase."

Tuttle stood beside Keegan and pointed at the ledger page. The column in which C. Amore stood was headed Name.

"It means With Love," Agnes said.

"And lamb means a baby sheep. What does Horvath mean?" he demanded of Cy.

"I don't know."

"Keegan probably means something too, back on the old sod. So what if Con Amore means With Love. There are D'Amores and Amours in the book. Those are names."

Tuttle spoke with urgency and eloquence. But Keegan could

see in his mind the ring they had found on the dead body of Aggie Miller. He could see the frozen body of Frances Grice lying in a canoe under ice. AG to FG. *Con amore.*

"Where did you hear of the ring, Tuttle? From Peanuts?"

"What ring?"

"The one with the inscription in it that includes Con Amore. It was Mrs. Grice's ring. Mrs. Aggie Miller bought it at a street sale in Elgin and was killed by someone trying to get it back."

Tuttle followed this recital with great attention, a smile forming on his thin lips. He took off his hat and banged it against his leg.

"I knew I was onto something! That proves it was the killer who rented the canoe."

The fact was, it made sense. Staring at the scrawl on the ledger page, Keegan wondered if that was the signature of the killer. "I suppose you handled the hell out of this page, Tuttle."

"No more than you have, Captain Keegan. Do you agree that I have a strong claim on that fifty thousand dollar reward?"

"I'd answer that but you'd call me as a witness."

"I'll be subpoenaing you in any case, Captain. And your colleagues. The testimony of Mr. Foley will be crucial. Fortunately confidentiality does not apply since, as you all heard, he is not my client." Tuttle threw out his arms as if to embrace the world. "Ladies and gentlemen, my ship has come in."

"They only have canoes here, Tuttle."

"And most of those without a paddle. Well, if I'm no longer needed . . ." He started for the door, then stopped and turned dramatically on his heel. "Captain, I rely on you to warn Mr. Grice that he harasses me at his peril."

"Explain that to him when he's knocking your block off."

"I will sue him out of his socks."

Agnes prepared to block Tuttle's way, but Keegan shook his head. In one fell swoop they had gained everything they could from Tuttle. Foley could tell them more of the ledger from which this page had been torn.

But a further hour spent with Foley and his dog made it clear that the summer employee and winter caretaker of the marina could cast no light on who had given his name as C. Amore and then scrawled *Con Amore* in the ledger.

Keegan was so preoccupied on the drive back that he forgot to tell Agnes where he wanted to go. Thus he was dropped off at his own apartment. Well, he would go on to the St. Hilary rectory in a while. First he went inside for a shower, and to pursue the line of thought that had begun in the backseat of the car.

They had a series of events difficult to account for by a single agent. First there was the kidnapping of Frances Grice, the stripping of her body of clothing and jewelry, with the inscribed ring ending in a street sale in Elgin. Where was everything else? The kidnapper disposed of the body in a canoe rented from the marina and sank it beneath the Grice boat house before the river began to freeze. That could have been just days after Mrs. Grice's disappearance, since the canoe was rented on September 28. Rented under a supposed name that pointed at the ring. Did the killer presume that the ring would be found? If what happened had not happened—the sale of the ring, its purchase by Aggie Miller—the only one who could have understood the name assumed by the renter of the canoe was Arthur Grice.

But the ring had been found and the inscription learned of by a small group of people at St. Hilary's parish center. Then the killer wanted the ring back and killed Aggie in an attempt to get it. Why?

As he reviewed these events, a specific figure was present in his mind, impossible to expel, yet equally impossible to think of as the perpetrator of the events so far recalled.

In the shower, he let the stinging stream play on the top of his head, as if it could drum new ideas into his skull. When he emerged from the shower, nude as the corpse of Frances Grice except that he was also shoeless, he rubbed steam from the mirror, leaned toward it and spoke aloud.

"Madeleva Haimu is Con Amore."

He repeated it in various tones, but no matter how he said it he could not believe it. And so the list continued. He thought of subsequent events as he put a meat pie in the microwave.

The telephone calls. The first one rustling him and others out of bed in order to find a shoe that had belonged to Frances Grice, the second leading to the body. Why would the killer draw attention to his or her deed (he sounded like a document coming from Chief Robertson's office, full of he or she and patrol persons and the like) when it was highly unlikely the body would have been discovered until late spring at the earliest? Had someone other than the murderer made those calls?

Phil Keegan saved the most baffling events for his drive to Father Dowling's.

There seemed no way in the world to avoid the probability that Madeleva Haimu had attempted to poison both Arthur Grice and Pamela Mathers. In these two cases they had a suspect in custody, ready to have formal charges brought against her in the morning. The prosecutor's office would be sorely tempted to try Madeleva for the poisonings while holding in abeyance the possibility of charges against her in the deaths of Aggie Miller and Frances Grice. There would be no need to establish the charges that were not brought. It was not a matter of influencing the jury, but the public would be invited to see all these events as a package. And that, in turn, would influence Robertson to order the cops to direct their energies somewhere else.

Phil Keegan didn't like it. It would be far better if they could pin the killings on Madeleva too, not just the attempted poisonings. If she went on trial for those alone, she or someone else might slip through the net of justice. Preventing that from happening had to be their first concern. Even if it meant having more than one suspect.

Twenty-Two

Madeleva Haimu broke her self-imposed silence two days after her arrest and demanded to see a priest. She wanted a Coptic priest, but after agreeing to at least meet with Father Dowling, and having sat silently across the table for five minutes staring at him with large, inscrutable eyes, she began to talk.

"I am a sinner, Father."

"We are all sinners."

"I tried to kill two people."

"Thank God you did not succeed."

"I cannot do that. My sorrow is for the fact that I failed."

"You wanted to kill Arthur Grice and Pamela?"

Her mouth widened in a smile, but only when her lips stretched wide did they open to reveal her great white teeth. "You see how you say their names together."

The priest waited, fearful that anything he said would bring the conversation to an end. He felt in the presence of an elemental female principle. Madeleva was seated and appeared relaxed, but her back was straight and did not seek the support of a chair. Her chin was tilted, and her fine-boned face with its enormous eyes, the extremely short-cut hair, and the earrings that seemed to glow in the lobes, all gave off the feeling of an earlier century.

"He is a man and married, but I had the fleshly desires nonetheless. I got down on my knees and promised God that I would not be a temptation to him. Men find me attractive. I know that. It has always been like that. It could have been like that with him. But I promised and I kept my promise. Then his wife disappeared."

"Someone killed her, Madeleva."

Her head moved slightly as if discouraging a fly. "Then it was more difficult for me. It was difficult for him too. But I had promised. I had failed to think of Pamela."

"How do you mean?"

"Pamela is an American."

"Yes."

"By that I mean she is a pagan. Women in this country . . ." She paused to think. Again, the slight movement of her head. "They are pagans."

"You think that Pamela . . ."

"It was in the newspapers," Madeleva said calmly. "It was common talk at the office. After I had denied myself, he allowed himself to be tempted by her."

Madeleva had taken the arsenic from the maintenance building at her condominium, where it was used for rats. As she spoke of it, it seemed a drama that had unfolded in a garden between the Tigris and Euphrates rivers, not the daily doings of ordinary people in Fox River, Illinois. But great tragedies are played out in improbable places. Madeleva and Arthur Grice had become Desdemona and Othello, at least in her mind, and quotidian actions had become freighted with life-and-death significance.

"Who killed Frances Grice?"

The question seemed to surprise Madeleva.

"It will be thought that you did. You tried to kill two other people. Did you kill Mrs. Grice as well."

"No."

"Did you kill Mrs. Miller?"

"No."

She might have been answering questions in order to obtain a driver's license. Even as he asked about Aggie Miller, Roger Dowling saw the inappropriateness of it. A large man had shoveled Aggie's walk and had somehow got into her house, where he had cut her throat.

"You didn't kill anyone, did you?"

Tears formed in her rounded eyes. "I am sorry."

"God will forgive you."

She sat straighter. "I am sorry that I failed."

After he left the jail, Roger Dowling took the elevator to the floor where Phil had his office.

"Can you tell me anything, Roger?"

"She didn't kill anyone."

"That's not her fault."

"She thinks it is."

Phil considered that, then shook his head. "I don't understand you and please don't explain." He picked up a half-smoked cigar and looked at it. "So it's back to Arthur Grice."

"You think he killed his wife?"

"Someone had to."

"But an attempt was made on his life."

"By someone who killed nobody. Look, Grice could have killed his wife and still been slipped a doctored Coke by a lovelorn secretary."

Remembering Madeleva's anguish, Roger found Phil's description of what Madeleva had gone through trivializing.

"Why would Arthur Grice kill his wife?"

"You think I'll say Pamela Mathers, don't you?"

"What was his motive?"

"Greed. Power. Independence."

Phil did not put it eloquently, but the phenomenon he described was familiar enough. His examples were those of celebrities. The man or woman becomes a star, then drops the spouse who made the climb with him or her. The wife works to send her husband through medical school, only to be abandoned when his practice becomes lucrative. The Grice version was a young couple who together had turned a dying family business into a regional phenomenon. Then the point was reached when Grice no longer wanted to share the credit with his wife.

"So he got rid of her. And he made it look good. He sold some of her jewelry at a street sale in Elgin, then killed the woman who bought a ring. He set us up with the shoe by the roadside and then revealed the body of his wife. It was just dumb luck that his secretary decided to poison him and Pamela . . ."

"Luck?"

"He tried to make himself look like a sorrowing husband being harassed by whoever murdered his wife."

It was clear from Phil's voice that a theory he had begun to develop in almost apologetic tones was getting a grip on him. Roger Dowling could sympathize with his desire to account for the deaths of Frances Grice and Aggie Miller, but the story had too many holes.

"And one major flaw."

"What?"

"How did he know Aggie Miller bought the ring?"

Phil stared at him for half a minute, then brought his hand down triumphantly on the desk.

"Because he sold it to her!"

That remotely plausible answer had the effect of commending the theory even more solidly to Phil Keegan. But Roger Dowling doubted it would survive a good night's sleep.

"Amos Cadbury the lawyer called," Marie said when he got back to the parish house. The temperature had risen and the melting snow created a slush that was kicked up by the tires of passing cars. Roger Dowling still stood in the doorway, stamping it off his shoes. Behind him, Forbes was ridding the walks of accumulated water with a large squeegee.

"What did he want?"

"He said you would know."

Roger hung up his topcoat and looked at Marie. The housekeeper was in a mood, no doubt about that. Marie prided herself on getting out of people what they intended to keep secret, but she had more than met her match in Amos Cadbury. The wily septuagenarian lawyer had been outwitting his fellow mortals for half a century.

"Does he want me to call him?"

"He didn't say."

"Did you ask him?"

"I just take down the messages I am given, Father Dowling. Far be it from me to pry into matters that do not concern me."

"Did Amos tell you to mind your own business?"

Her mouth dropped open as an expression of shock spread over her face. "Mr. Amos Cadbury is a gentleman, Father Dowling. He would never insult a lady."

She turned, threw back her shoulders and marched into her kitchen. Roger Dowling was used to losing such obscure battles, but since he had no idea what was at stake in them he did not mind. He went into his study and dialed Amos Cadbury's number. A bright-voiced receptionist put him through to Amos's secretary, whose chilled tones thawed when she realized the receptionist's mistake.

"Father, how are you? The girl said a Mr. Dowling was on the line and of course I did not think it could possibly be you."

"I haven't been laicized, Irene."

"Oh good heavens, don't even say it. I'll put you through to Mr. Cadbury."

A moment later the sepulchral voice of Amos Cadbury said, "Congratulations, Father Dowling. I am told you have already been informed of your good fortune."

Roger Dowling looked across the room at the five-volume set of the *Summa Theologiae* ranged upon a shelf.

"Could you remind me, Amos."

"Willis Wirth has left St. Hilary's a gift of fifty thousand dollars."

"Yes, of course. The Lorings did tell me that."

"Most irregular. In any case, I shall insist on doing things in the proper way. Can you come to my office, Father, or would you prefer that I come to the rectory?"

"It would seem ungrateful not to be willing to come downtown for that amount of money."

"Actually I would not mind in the least coming by the rectory. I could stop there on my way home. Unless, of course . . ."

"Amos, I welcome the opportunity to get out of the house."

After he hung up, Marie walked past the door, very swiftly, studiously ignoring him, obviously unconcerned with any telephone calls the pastor might be making.

"I just talked with Amos Cadbury."

No answer, but she came to a halt.

"Despite your rudeness he will hand over the fifty thousand dollars."

Marie appeared in the doorway, a look of outrage fading.

"Fifty thousand dollars?"

"Try to be nice to him when he phones."

She assumed a haughty look. "I hope I know how to do my job, Father."

"So do I."

"You're trying to make me mad but it won't work."

Roger Dowling nodded and picked up his pipe. "Fifty thousand dollars will buy a lot of snowblowers."

Marie marched back to her kitchen and slammed the door vigorously.

Twenty-Three

Over a long and lucrative lifetime in the law, Amos Cadbury's conception of the point of his profession had altered radically but so gradually it came almost as a surprise to him to realize how he approached his task.

In his callow youth, just out of the Notre Dame law school, imbued with the notion of an unwritten or natural law that is the measure of the justice of men, he had thought of what he did in terms of high moral seriousness. The practice of law eroded that idea, and he accepted the implications of the adversarial conception without realizing what he was doing. If he defended a client's innocence, another lawyer was just as zealously trying to establish that client's guilt. The fact that Amos might just as easily argue one side of the case as the other weakened the notion that counselors and court sought the just and correct answer. Eventually the answer decided on *was* the right answer—the legal answer.

Thus sapped of its substance, the law retained the allure of rigorous procedure, and this had become Amos's sustaining idea of what he did. It was no longer a matter of asking whether what had been done correctly was just; justice was simply doing things according to the rules. Amos became an almost pathological stickler for details. He was the lawyer you wanted when you drew up a contract. He was a lawyer to whom you could entrust your will with every confidence that it would be executed precisely as you had wished. That had been Willis Wirth's expectation, and Amos Cadbury intended to carry out his late client's provisions with a meticulous attention to detail, no matter what he personally might think of some of the provisions of the will.

It seemed disloyal to the faith he had learned from his mother's knee to say that he had preferred Willis as he had been before his conversion to Catholicism. Not that Amos would say that, but he certainly thought it. Leaving one's money to surviving relatives was unquestionably the thing to do, and leaving it in the correct proportions in terms of closeness of kinship. Amos had no quarrel with that part of Willis Wirth's will, which was the bulk of it, governing two million dollars. But the pious bequests went against the grain of Amos's notion of why one accumulated money in the first place. Two hundred thousand dollars to Mother Angelica, a nun engaged in television work! Even the fifty thousand dollars to St. Hilary's parish brought the suggestion of a frown to Amos's patrician features. St. Hilary's was the parish of his youth. He had been married in its church. It was all too easy to see the Fox River area in which the parish stood with nostalgia and sentiment, but cool reason told him that the area and the parish were doomed. He had little doubt that someday soon four lanes of traffic would roar across the spot on which he had given his hand and heart to the woman who had been his companion for almost fifty-five years.

Such thoughts went through Amos Cadbury's mind during the three unscheduled minutes he sat at his desk before seeing Roger Dowling. The priest was not late for his appointment. It was Amos's practice to have a few moments before each professional encounter in which to review what lay ahead. But, since he anticipated no difficulties with Roger Dowling, he had permitted himself the indulgence of rumination.

"Let me say at the outset that I am embarrassed by this," Father Dowling said, after they had shaken hands and settled down in a corner of the office in facing chairs.

"Money honestly come by is not an embarrassment."

"Then you have hit on the source of mine. I feel that Willis was governed by his heart rather than his head."

"You realize the money was left to the parish?"

"Of course."

"Surely you will find some good use for it."

"Money is meant to be spent, isn't it? There are a number of things we can do with it. But none of them is really necessary."

Amos managed not to wince at the heretical notion that money should be spent. He preferred to think of money as fertile, to be gathered and kept in the dark where it could busily pullulate and reproduce itself.

"What is necessary from my point of view is to fulfill the wishes of Willis Wirth."

Father Dowling nodded. Amos was pleased that he did not seem to regard this as a pious remark, but merely expressive of what was genuinely of the essence.

"Of course. I understand that the gift to the parish will not deprive his heirs."

"Willis provided for them generously."

"The Lorings?"

"Mr. Loring will have cause for no further complaints so far as money is concerned."

Amos watched the priest as he spoke, and he was delighted that Father Dowling understood. Not many laymen grasped the fact that the slightest linguistic turn can carry large implications.

"Further?"

"Perhaps all businessmen complain."

"Certainly building contractors do. My father was one. Not that he did as well as Paul Loring."

"I wonder. He would have lived when money was available at more reasonable rates. Mr. Loring has been the target of several punitive lawsuits. His insurance costs are truly astronomical."

"I didn't realize that."

"Perhaps this will sound disloyal, Father Dowling, but I think there are too many lawyers."

"I wish I could say the same of priests."

"I have heard it said that, few as there are now, there still may be too many priests as well."

To Amos's relief, Roger Dowling laughed. Amos had always concealed how appalled he was at the changes that had taken place in the Catholic Church. He did not want to think about them let alone discuss them, it was so painful.

"You may be right, Amos. I mean about lawyers, of course."

Amos had been a key figure in the local bar association for years, but of late he had not been standing for committee appointments. The law was not what it had been. Nor were lawyers. He thought of the ineffable Tuttle. Twice he had voted to disbar that rascal and twice he had been overridden by lawyers scarcely more ethical than Tuttle. A few days ago Tuttle had telephoned and announced he was representing Arthur Grice, and had the temerity to suggest that they have a conference! Amos had suffered this in silence. He would no more inquire of Grice about this betrayal than he would schedule a conference with Tuttle.

"The custom, Father Dowling, is for me to read the will to you."

"Is that necessary?"

"It is how it is done."

After the slightest of pauses the priest said, "Then that is how we must do it."

It was not quite accurate to claim that a complete reading of the will to each beneficiary was customary, but Amos had decided it was the best way to convey certain facts to Roger Dowling without seeming to divulge what the priest had no need to know.

Amos took a sip of water and began to read. He did so with pleasant memories of writing these sentences and of lengthy sessions with Willis Wirth, refurbishing and changing, adding and subtracting, getting things precisely as Willis wished. What a delight he had been to work with, despite his unsettling habit of asking questions about transubstantiation and the hypostatic union. These had driven Amos to his catechism, for which perhaps he should be grateful.

The prologue to the will was unusually long, since Willis had insisted on addressing the deity at great length and informing him of things he should be presumed to know already.

There followed his philanthropic bequests, among which was the fifty thousand dollar gift to St. Hilary parish. This was a point at which Amos might have stopped reading, but he went on.

Audrey Wirth Loring and her second cousin Frances were to share equally in some two million dollars. Amos had opposed this in every way he knew—gently, firmly, almost angrily—but Willis had been adamant. It would have been far better to leave his daughter a larger portion.

"I already told her," Willis had replied.

"What did she say?"

"I just told her fifty-fifty. She probably hasn't the faintest idea how much money we're talking about."

In Amos's experience, heirs usually had a far better than faint idea how much money might come their way. He wished Willis had kept quiet about the distribution. He wished this even more after Mr. Loring came to see him.

This was the son-in-law whose pleas for infusions of cash

into his business, for loans against the future inheritance, had fallen on deaf ears.

"If he can't make it without a rich relative, he deserves to fail," Willis had said.

"I hope you didn't say that to him."

"He got the point, Amos."

Money is a great equalizer. Money had enabled the fragile Willis to scold the hulking, powerful Paul Loring, and give him sermons about proper business procedure.

"He should stop comparing himself to the big boys and do what he can do."

By the big boys Willis had meant Grice Enterprises. What irony that Loring's chief business rival should be married to Audrey's second cousin, and scheduled to inherit an equal amount.

No need to spell out this irony to Father Dowling. Amos Cadbury had rarely seen a more attentive listener. Even people who were hearing themselves become rich did not always pay heed to the details of a will. But Father Dowling followed with unfeigned interest these refined details of the will of the late Willis Wirth.

Twenty-Four

When Roger Dowling left Amos Cadbury's office, he entered a crowded elevator, returned one or two tentative nods, and dropped with his companions to ground level. My feet fly down, my thoughts remain above. The reading of the will had suggested something and he meant to check on it immediately.

From a phone booth in the lobby, he called Loring Construction and was told that Mr. Loring was on a building site.

"Where exactly is it?"

"Who's calling, please?"

"Roger Dowling. Father Dowling. I buried his father-in-law." An odd identification, but he did not want to be put off. The woman told him in altered tones how he could find the house under construction on the shores of King Lake.

"I hope he's still there when I get there."

"He will be." Then she added, "We're behind schedule with that house and Mr. Loring is there a lot."

On the drive to King Lake, Roger let the thoughts come. He

had seen Paul Loring often enough of late, but the image that filled his mind was that of Loring when he'd come into the waiting room of Riverview Nursing Home, stomping the snow off his boots and looking somewhat less than kindly at Roger Dowling.

It had not occurred to him then that the Lorings were the heirs of Willis Wirth, but even if it had, it would have meant little, since he had no idea of how wealthy Willis was. The prospect of that money combined with a business in need of cash did something to explain the scarcely concealed impatience of the Lorings with the time it had taken Willis to shuffle off this mortal coil.

Frances Morin. That was how Audrey's cousin had been named in the will.

"Half?"

Amos nodded. "Willis insisted. The girl's mother was his only sister."

"Where does she live?"

"She's a local girl."

It was with the sense of playing twenty questions that he went on. "Married?"

"To a man named Grice."

Amos got slowly to his feet as he said it and then stood erect, hand extended. The meeting was over.

"I shall have the money transferred to the parish account, if that is satisfactory."

"Whom do I thank?"

"Your benefactor is gone."

"And he is already in my prayers."

"That is what he would have wanted, Father. I assure you."

"I think you're right."

Now, trying to keep back the thoughts surging into his mind, he said the name aloud. Frances Grice. Co-heir with Audrey to the Wirth fortune. Without children, without an heir of her own, the cousin's money would revert to Audrey and her husband.

The directions he had been given took him through an established residential development to a back road that twisted away through an unspoiled wood. Rural mailboxes at infrequent intervals testified to the existence of homes hidden from the road. A discrete sign announced the presence of Loring Construction, and Father Dowling swung off the road and parked. None too soon. The railroad-tie abutment was incomplete, and when he got out of his car he looked down into a deep ravine through which a ribbon of ice suggested a stream.

Boards had been laid out over the snow, slush, and clay, as a walkway to the house, a vast angular thing whose windows seemed disproportionately small. He came to a stop by a rusty steel barrel, cut away to make an improvised stove. Lathes and board ends had been tossed out of the house to be used as fuel, but at present the fire consisted of a couple of smoldering logs. There were several pickup trucks, one with oversize wheels whose tires had massive treads. A ramplike walk led up to what would eventually be the front door. Roger Dowling walked slowly up it, waiting to be challenged, ready to identify himself. But he went unhailed, and apparently unnoticed, inside

The smell of new wood filled his nostrils. Plasterboard bearing its manufacturer's label like garish wallpaper adorned the room, windows cut into it, unevenly edged. The windows facing the lake were huge, and the glass had already been installed. There was a vast two-way fireplace in a massive arrow-shaped room at whose point two picture windows met, and a strip of brown paper on which to walk.

"Who're you looking for?"

Roger Dowling turned around and looked up. From a balcony Paul Loring looked down at him, his expression reminiscent of the one that had remained in the priest's memory from the Riverview. Would he have recognized him otherwise? He wore a cap and a denim coat, dusty with plaster. The heads of nails emerged from his lips.

"Roger Dowling."

An impatient nod. "What can I do for you?"

"Can I come up there?"

"Be careful on the stairs."

The stairs, obviously temporary, consisted of a rising scale of boards, no risers, flanked by a flimsy railing nailed to a four-by-four that served as post. Roger Dowling was uneasily aware that the stairs passed over a well that dropped into the basement, from which rose the musky smell of still-wet cement. He was not afflicted with acrophobia; on the other hand, he had a natural fear of heights. He lifted his chin, tried not to think of the fragile look of the stairs, and went up them as rapidly as he could. He gripped the railing, but when it wobbled under the pressure of his hand he let go. That railing was no protection at all. A similarly thin board was nailed into place in the upper hall, temporary placeholder for the permanent railing. What had Amos said of Loring's insurance? Roger could imagine accidents galore on such a site.

"What do you think of it, Father?" Loring meant the house.

"It's interesting."

"Would you want to live in it? I wouldn't. Except for the lake. The view is great. As for the house, I build what the client wants."

"I have just come from Amos Cadbury's office."

"You get a nice view of the living room from here," Loring said, taking Roger Dowling to the balcony from which he had called down.

"I like the smell of wood and cement."

Loring had taken the nails from his mouth, but he still held a hammer. "I no longer notice it. I suppose it's the same with you and incense."

"Willis has made you a millionaire, I understand."

"Did Amos tell you that?"

"He read the will to me."

"The money goes to my wife." He looked around. "It will ease the pressure. The construction business has been a roller coaster for the past several years."

"Will you continue?"

"I'm not retirement age, Father."

"I meant that you would have no more reason to work."

His jaw hardened and he looked with narrow eyes down the hallway of the house. "Now I'll be able to work the way I've wanted to. This house? Peanuts. The owner, the architect, all their relatives, are constantly wanting to alter the plans. What I would like to tell them and what I can afford to tell them are two very different things."

"I was surprised to learn that Mrs. Loring had a cousin."

"What's unusual about that?" He pushed back from the railing. Outside an engine started, and then another. Loring looked at his watch and shook his head. "That's another thing. When you know what you have to do, try and get construction workers who know how to follow orders."

"Who will get her money?"

"You'd have to ask Amos that."

"Don't you know?"

Loring started down the hall, and Roger Dowling followed him. Loring went into a room where there was a trestle table, stacks of plasterboard, and an electric saw. He began to nail sections of wallboard in place.

"You look as if you could build the house yourself."

"And probably save money doing it." The rhythmic bang of the hammer echoed in the enclosed space. The window in the wall was still just a rectangular hole opening on a woodsy scene.

When he finished nailing, Loring wrestled a length of plasterboard onto the table, positioned it, and turned on the saw. It was a rasping, irritating sound, and Loring seemed to prolong the racket by moving the saw slowly down a penciled line. When the sound stopped, Roger Dowling could have cheered.

"Can I help you?" he asked when Loring took hold of the board.

"Better not, Father."

He levered it up, turned and lifted it precisely into place, pressed it home with his knee, took a nail from his mouth and drove it home. Two or three more and he turned.

"You can see what it does?" He indicated the chalk marks on his denim jacket left by the wallboard.

"You obviously don't need help."

"On a job, it's always best to work out ways of doing anything on your own. Chances are you'll have to eventually."

"It was what I said that told you where the ring was, wasn't it?"

The hammer, poised to strike, did not move. "What ring?" The words seemed filtered through the nails, metallic, cold.

"The ring Aggie Miller bought in Elgin."

"You're not making sense." Loring began to nail, seemingly with new force, as if he would drive the nails into the next dimension.

"Why did you sell it?"

The hammering continued, more nails than necessary being driven into the border of the plasterboard.

"Whether or not you sold it yourself, you had not counted on it turning up so close to home. Why, Aggie had known you as a boy. How many pieces did you sell in order that one might be turned in as a clue?"

Loring turned and got another length onto the trestle. "Go on,"- he said, but then he turned on the saw. He looked at Roger Dowling from behind the shield of noise. The round blade continued to whir long after the piece he had sawed off fell to the floor. Finally he turned it off.

"Go on," he urged again.

"I think you know perfectly well where the money Willis Wirth left Frances Grice would go, if she were dead."

"To her husband."

"Your great rival. But if he were convicted of killing his wife . . ."

"You mean committed suicide?"

"The best-laid plans."

"You're wrong if you think I poisoned Grice's Coke."

"Oh, you didn't plan to get rid of him. Poor Arthur Grice, you wanted more than his life. You wanted to destroy his reputation as well, didn't you? Make him a murderer who could not inherit. Two birds at once, the money and his name."

"Don't feel sorry for that son of a bitch."

"Oh, I don't. He will be able to enjoy Willis's money. You won't."

Loring grinned, but it was a cruel grin. "A citizen's arrest? Read me the charges."

"You killed Frances Grice and buried her underwater in the boat house, having stripped her and removed one of her shoes. You meant to enjoy what you were doing. To lead the police to Arthur Grice and to the body, if necessary. No doubt, as with the ring, you assumed it would be discovered and fuel suspicion of Arthur Grice. When through my stupidity you learned that the ring was here in Fox River, you decided to repossess it. You killed Aggie Miller but did not get the ring."

"I hope you haven't told this nonsense to anyone else."

"Your trail is an obvious one. The will is all anyone needs to begin to see what happened."

"Did you talk to Amos?"

"Paul, it's over. Is there a phone here? No, of course there wouldn't be. Come with me now to talk with Captain Keegan."

"You're serious, aren't you?"

"Yes."

Loring stared at the priest, but his eyes seemed unfocused. "I was an altar boy when I was a kid."

"Were you?"

"Cassock, surplice, the whole bit. I used to like Benediction and carrying the censer, swinging it, making the puffs of smoke rise."

"God can forgive anything, Paul. Even murder."

This seemed to wake him from dreams of innocence to the reality of his present. His expression firmed and he flicked his thumb. The saw began to whine. Holding it in front of him, he came around the table toward Roger Dowling.

Roger stepped back and stumbled on the stack of plaster-board, losing his balance and pitching to the floor. He rolled away from the ear-shattering sound, trying to get to his feet. He looked back just as Loring lunged toward him with the whirling saw. The priest inhaled a gasping breath as if it were his last, and closed his eyes.

The noise stopped abruptly. Roger opened his eyes. Loring swung around, toward the room in which he had been working. He had pulled the plug from the wall. Thank God, it was not battery driven. Roger, on his feet, slipped into the open door of the next room. A moment later, Loring thundered past.

The footsteps ceased. Silence. Was he going to come back? The sense of resignation he had felt when Loring had tried to push the whirling saw blade into his back was gone. He looked around for something with which to defend himself.

"Father Dowling." It was Loring, calling softly. "Father Dowling, where are you?"

They might have been playing hide and seek. There was nothing in the room that could serve as a weapon.

"Fa-ther Dow-ling."

The coaxing voice was no nearer. Roger eased his back against the wall, and moved slowly toward the door. When he looked out he saw Loring, the hammer in his hand, leaning out over the stairwell. Against the wall was a two-by-four the length of a baseball bat. Roger Dowling tiptoed from the room, took the board and moved behind Loring, bringing the board back and gripping it with both hands. Putting his body into it, he swung at his target—the wrist of the arm with which Loring held the hammer.

Loring let out a roar of pain as the board struck. The hammer fell, bouncing several times on the steps as it descended. Wheeling around, Loring grasped his wrist, his face twisted with rage. The sudden motion threw him off balance and he tried to catch himself, but teetered backward. His back struck the makeshift railing, which snapped like a twig. For a timeless moment he seemed suspended over the stairwell, staring wild-eyed at Roger Dowling. And then he fell. Soundlessly. Until there was a great crash, then a series of wrenching sounds as the temporary staircases broke under his weight. Roger Dowling leaned over to see the huge man at the mercy of gravity crashing through the stairs and then, as he stared upward, continuing into the basement.

That was when Paul Loring screamed.

A bloody pointed stick emerged from the left side of his chest, growing longer and longer as Paul Loring became impaled on it.

Twenty-Five

I n late February Roger Dowling and Phil Keegan sat in the rectory study watching the Bulls play the Celtics. The room was heavy with cigar and pipe smoke, Phil was drinking his third beer, and Roger Dowling, who had asked for coffee, was drinking cocoa. What housekeeper, when her pastor asks for coffee, will reach him a cup of cocoa? Marie Murkin, that's who. She was punishing him for excluding her from the dinner-table conversation that had turned on the prosecutor's decision not to indict Madeleva Haimu.

"You might lace it with a little arsenic, Marie," Phil said dryly. "That's not a criminal offense in this state."

"Attempting it isn't a criminal offense," Roger Dowling corrected.

Marie would not be baited. It was far too late for the two of them to make amends, her manner suggested. She behaved as if her hearing had suddenly failed and, waving a pathway through the hovering smoke, she left the study.

"It makes a mockery out of police work," Phil said.

"It is the prosecutor who is being criticized."

Mervel had written a column listing the unsolved crimes that had plagued Fox River. This was a prelude to his expression of outrage that a woman who had tried to poison her employer and her coworker was free to walk the streets like any citizen.

"Yeah? Is that why he suggested people are stepping over bodies on every street in town?"

The murders of Frances Grice and Aggie Miller were technically still under investigation, but not even Cy Horvath seemed confident that the murderer would be found. It was painful to Roger Dowling to know what he knew and to keep it from his old friend. But he had told no one of the conversation that had preceded Paul Loring's fatal fall in the unfinished house on King Lake. It would have been stretching a point beyond recognition to say that his silence was due to professional confidentiality, let alone the seal of the confessional. He had given Loring absolution, of course, and there was still a pulse in his neck when he did so. But blood had gushed from the wound with such rapidity and in such quantity that it was clear the heart itself had been punctured. Was Loring conscious when the same blessing was given him that had so recently been given Willis Wirth?

How the two deaths differed, yet how related they were. On the verge of becoming a rich man, Paul Loring had tried to double the inheritance by murdering Frances Grice and framing her husband and heir. Thus, Arthur Grice would not have been allowed to inherit.

The controlling reason for Roger Dowling's silence had been the realization that nothing would be gained by speaking up. The lives of Frances Grice and Aggie Miller could not be restored, nor could the man responsible for their deaths be punished, at least not on this side of the grave. His name would be uselessly ruined, which would cause yet more pain to Audrey, who had lost her husband close on the heels of losing her father. Being a wealthy widow was no immediate consolation.

"Dad meant for Frances to have half, Father."

"So Amos Cadbury told me."

"He did?"

"Because your father left that money to St. Hilary's. Amos has the practice of reading the will to each benefactor . . ."

"Be careful."

"How do you mean?"

"Inheriting money from my father is a dangerous business. First Frances, then Paul."

Was he surprised that she had not the least suspicion that her husband had done what he had? He tried to imagine her reaction if he divulged what he knew to be the truth.

"It's funny the things you worry about, Father."

"How so?"

"I always worried about Paul's boating. I hate water and he was often out alone."

"On the river?"

"Yes. He'd known it since he was a kid. His dream was to have a house on the river, a boat house. A house like the Grices'."

"Ah."

When Roger Dowling went down to the marina and stood looking across at the Grices' pier and boat house, an old fellow and his dog came out on the dock.

"Afternoon, Father. Can I help you?"

It was Foley and his dog. Roger Dowling had heard from Phil of Cy's shanghaiing Foley for his trip across the river. The custodian nodded sagely when the priest mentioned Frances Grice.

"It was one of our canoes, Father. They found the body in a sunken canoe and darned if it wasn't one of ours."

"Rented from the marina?"

"More likely stolen."

Foley showed him where the canoes were stacked in season. Not that he thought it would have been all that easy to steal a canoe. Even if there had been no one on the dock itself, getting to the dock would have meant going by at least two people.

"So you figure the thief came from the river side?"

Foley thought about it, perhaps for the first time. He liked the idea.

"It had to be, Father. Someone could just pull up to the dock and slide a canoe into the water. Nothing to it. You wouldn't think someone in a boat would steal a canoe, but it's the best explanation."

Looking out at the river, its channel bordered by ice, Roger imagined Paul Loring taking the canoe, putting the nude body of Frances Grice into it, sinking it, and pushing it into the Grice boat house. Audrey had told him Paul often boated late into the night and was reluctant to admit the season was over. How often had he seen the Grice estate from the river and fed his envy on the sight?

Was it really unfair to Phil not to present him with information that mightn't prove convincing enough to a prosecutor even if Loring were still alive? Phil and Cy were better off without information that could only add to their difficulties and would not lighten their burden.

Thus at any rate thought Roger Dowling, and it was far from the first time that he had had to carry in silence knowledge of the sins of others.

"What does Agnes think of Madeleva's good fortune?"

"She says it will give affirmative action a bad name."

"Better not send her out for Cokes, Phil."

"Send Agnes for Cokes? You're kidding."

A sound in the hall indicated that Marie had crept from the kitchen to monitor their conversation.

"What wonderful cocoa!" he said in a slightly raised voice. "You're kidding."

"Phil, Marie really needs someone to look after."

"Yeah." Phil stirred in his chair but kept his eyes on the TV. "She's got you."

"It's not enough. I think she's in love."

"Anyone I know?"

"I think so."

The very silence from the hallway seemed audible.

"Who?"

"Do you know the big fellow who shovels the walks?"

A sputtering sound from the hallway was followed by the slamming of the kitchen door.

"What was that?" Phil asked.

"The kitchen door, I think."

"You should get it fixed." But Phil was watching Larry Bird loft a three-point shot from three feet outside the circle.

Phil had been surprised and happy to hear of the bequest Willis Wirth had made the parish.

"He made a number of surprising bequests."

That was as close as Roger had come to providing Phil with the wherewithal for discovering that Paul Loring had had a motive to kill Frances Grice.

"I was as surprised as anyone."

"You and Tuttle."

Amos Cadbury had the humbling task of paying Tuttle the reward Arthur Grice had offered for information that would be instrumental in finding the one who had tried to kill his wife. Foley had signed an affidavit on Tuttle's behalf, and so had Horowitz. The page from the ledger was the basis for the claim that if the police knew how to do their work it would be a small matter to track down C. Amore. It fell to Amos Cadbury to persuade Grice to pay off the lawyer in order to avoid prolonged and harassing lawsuits. Cadbury offered Tuttle ten thousand, speaking to him on the telephone, eyes shut, as if he did not want to witness what he himself was doing. Tuttle demanded twenty. They settled on fifteen.

"I'll be in your office in ten minutes."

An alarmed Amos assured Tuttle that a special messenger would have the certified check in his hands in scarcely more time than that.

"It was hard enough to do, Father Dowling. But to have had to recommend it to Mr. Grice as well." Amos's eyes lifted. "The claim seemed less than strong."

"Did it?"

"You think he had a right to the money?"

"What I paid for, Father Dowling, was silence, a closing of the books. Of course I took possession of the page torn from the ledger. You know where any more publicity might have led."

So Amos had known. Not that the lawyer could have been induced to say it in so many words. His professional code required divulgence rather than the opposite. Roger Dowling had no doubt that Amos had devised an elaborate rationale for what he was doing. Besides, the money came from what Willis Wirth had left Frances Grice. Perhaps the lawyer reasoned that he was protecting his late client's daughter.

"God writes with crooked lines," the priest said to Amos Cadbury.

"So do men, Father Dowling. So do men."